LUCY ... AN... DAN...G COMPETITION

All girls wishing to improve their dancing and their chances in local or national dancing festivals are invited to take a two-week dancing course (tap, ballet, modern and jazz included) at the Belle Adroit Summer Dancing Camp in Cornwall . . .

the announcement had said. So as soon as she got home that night, Lucy Jane said to her mother, 'Julie's and Jasmine's mums may be sending them to summer dance camp to help them to do better in the Golden Star Dancing Festival.' She paused, and then added, 'I'd like to go too, Mummy, if you'll let me. If we can all go it would be wonderful.'

Will Lucy Jane be able to go to the camp? And when her brother gets mumps, will it prevent her entering the Festival?

Also by Susan Hampshire

LUCY JANE AT THE BALLET
LUCY JANE ON TELEVISION

LUCY JANE AND THE DANCING COMPETITION

Susan Hampshire

Illustrated by Honey de Lacey

MAMMOTH

This book is dedicated to four friends
who are Lucy Jane followers:

Catherine Konliakidis
Kate McEnery
Georgina Broome
and Delia Kulukundis

My grateful thanks to Honey de Lacey for her lively
drawings which bring Lucy Jane to life so
beautifully.

Many thanks, too, especially to Sheila Hoad for
typing the first draft and also to Maureen Defries
and Kate Alden-Smith for patiently typing the
subsequent drafts.

And most important of all, a million thanks to
Miriam Hodgson, for whose guidance I am
extremely grateful. And last, but not least,
to my husband Eddie for his continued interest
in Lucy Jane.

First published in Great Britain 1991
by Methuen Children's Books Ltd
Published 1992 by Mammoth
an imprint of Mandarin Paperbacks
Michelin House, 81 Fulham Road, London SW3 6RB

Mandarin is an imprint of the Octopus Publishing Group,
a division of Reed International Books Ltd

Text copyright © 1991 by Susan Hampshire
Illustrations copyright © 1991 by Honey de Lacey

ISBN 0 7497 0979 0

A CIP catalogue record for this title
is available from the British Library

Printed in Great Britain
by Cox & Wyman Ltd, Reading, Berkshire

Contents

1 The Surprise 7

2 Accident 13

3 The Exam 23

4 Waiting 30

5 The Decision 39

6 Old Friends 50

7 The Very Important Guest 60

8 Telling the Truth 72

9 The Gift 83

10 The Setback 93

11 The Competition 103

12 The Results 118

1

The Surprise

Lucy Jane Tadworth never imagined she would enjoy anything so much as appearing in the *Nutcracker* ballet at Covent Garden, or find anything as exciting as playing Isabella in the television film *The Russell Adventure*. But she was mistaken, a new surprise was in store for her.

It all started one Wednesday afternoon at her school ballet lesson. Lucy Jane was lucky as her school encouraged music, painting and dancing. Miss Sweetfoot, the dancing teacher, suddenly said, 'Hands up those girls who want to enter the Golden Star Dancing Festival Competition. It is to be held at the Royal Albert Hall in the autumn with four famous judges.'

As Lucy Jane put her hand up a buzzy feeling went through her stomach. She hoped that there wouldn't be too many hands up or she might not have a chance to enter. Miss Sweetfoot counted and said, 'Five girls in this class, good. Now,' she said with a twinkle, 'which of you is prepared to work hard enough to take

their next ballet exam at the end of this term so that you are allowed to enter the competition?'

Again, Lucy Jane and her new best friend Jasmine put up their hands.

'Excellent,' Miss Sweetfoot said. 'All the girls doing the exam come to see me after the class. But,' she added, 'only those who *do well* in their ballet exam will be allowed to enter the festival.'

Lucy Jane squeezed Jasmine's hand excitedly. 'Just think, Jasmine, we may be able to do both. Hurray!' And she skipped around in a little circle until Miss Sweetfoot said, 'Come along, girls, on with the class.' Immediately, all the girls stood up straight and took their positions at the barre to start their *pliés* and *battements tendues*.

And that was how the new adventure for Lucy Jane began.

Most days after school Lucy Jane would go up to her room, move her bedroom furniture to one side and practise pointing her feet and stretching her instep to improve her point in front of the mirror. Then she would hold on to her dressing-table chair, and do the exercises she liked the least like *grande battement*. Lifting her leg high, while keeping her foot well pointed and trying to keep her back straight and her arm well positioned, was very hard. After about ten of these 'kicks', as her mother called them, on each side, Lucy Jane was usually fairly tired.

But today, Lucy Jane went straight into the kitchen and said to Mrs Tadworth, who was preparing the tea, 'Mummy, I can't do my homework after tea as I've got to practise for my ballet exam. If I pass I'm going to enter a dancing competition at the Albert Hall.' Her mother didn't have time to answer as Jeremy said, 'Jem, Jem dance too.' Lucy Jane's little brother was smiling up at her. Jeremy was nearly two.

But before Lucy Jane had time to say, 'Yes, Jeremy, you can dance too,' her mother said firmly, 'No, no, after tea you'll sit down and do your French homework and then when I put Jeremy to bed you can do your practice.'

So Lucy Jane reluctantly agreed. Suddenly she heard her father arriving home. She put down the list of French verbs and rushed to the door.

'Daddy, guess what?' She hugged him. 'I'm going to take my next ballet exam, Grade IV, and if I pass I'm going to enter the Golden Star Dancing Festival. It's a competition at the Albert Hall.'

'That sounds very grand,' her father said as he took off his coat, and although he was extremely tired from work he was happy to hear Lucy Jane's exciting news. He knew dancing meant so much to her. He was a set designer for television, his sister was wardrobe supervisor at Covent Garden*, so it seemed natural that Lucy Jane had always loved ballet and music ever since she was a little girl.

* See *Lucy Jane at the Ballet*

Lucy Jane took her ballet seriously. Sometimes in the mornings she would put on her leotard and ballet shoes before breakfast and do her *barre* exercises and practise her feet and arm positions.

'I must keep my elbows rounded,' she said to herself. 'Miss Sweetfoot said I mustn't let my thumbs stick out.' So many things to remember, so many things to improve before the exam. 'I have to pass,' she said, 'I so want to be in the Golden Star Festival.'

So Lucy Jane continued to work hard. As the day of the exam drew near Miss Sweetfoot said, 'Lucy Jane, I hope you will do well in the exam. I have high hopes for you if you can enter the Festival.'

In fact, Miss Sweetfoot had high hopes for Lucy Jane *and* Jasmine. She prayed that nothing would go wrong between now and the exam.

2

Accident

The morning of the exam Lucy Jane was out of bed long before the birds had even begun chirping in the trees.

'If it's raining,' she said to herself, as she put her slippers on, 'I'll pass the exam.'

But when she drew the curtains, she was too frightened to look outside, in case it was *not* raining. So she closed her eyes. It had rained for the past week, but today the early morning sun was glowing behind the chimney pots on the other side of the green. When Lucy Jane dared to look, she let out a little yelp of shock. 'Rabbits, I'll never pass the exam now,' she said feeling very worried, and she rushed out of the room to collect her ballet clothes that were drying in the bathroom. 'Why does the sun have to shine today?' she thought, as she ran downstairs to iron the ribbons on her ballet shoes. Her feet skipped from step to step so lightly that her slippered feet hardly touched the carpet. Suddenly, she slipped and cried, 'Oops, oh no!' as she missed the last step and found herself falling

to the floor in a heap at the bottom of the stairs. She was too shocked to speak, and immediately got to her feet. But when she tried to run into the kitchen she cried out in pain and had to bend down and hold her ankle. When she stood up and tried to walk again, she couldn't.

'Oh, Mummy,' she said to herself. 'I can't move, my foot hurts too much.' Lucy Jane's mother, father and brother were still fast asleep upstairs and didn't hear her plaintive little cries.

Suddenly she realised she couldn't dance or take her exam and she was so afraid, she shouted, 'Mummy, please help. My exam.' Again she rubbed her ankle more fiercely, wishing she hadn't been so foolish as to rush downstairs without looking.

Now Lucy Jane shouted even louder, 'Mummy!' until Mrs Tadworth came down to find her.

'Lucy, darling, what's the matter? Why are you crying?'

'I got up early to practise and iron my ribbons.' She hugged her mother and whispered, in a small voice, 'And I've hurt my foot.'

As she stood up to show her mother her foot she nearly fell over again, and now the tears poured down her cheeks. The hope of being in the Golden Star Dancing Festival seemed to be fast disappearing. What would Jasmine and the other girls say? They had promised each other that they would *all be there* on the big day at the Albert Hall.

'If only it was *raining*,' Lucy Jane continued dramatically.

'Don't be silly, Lucy. Why on earth do you want it to rain?' her mother asked as she looked out of the window, noticing the splashes of rain on the window pane.

'Because if it rains, I'll pass,' Lucy Jane answered, before her mother had time to tell her it was raining. Mrs Tadworth smiled to herself. 'What a silly little lamb you are. What nonsense. Now let's look at your foot.'

Lucy Jane's foot was very swollen and Mrs Tadworth wasn't sure at this point if Lucy Jane had twisted, bruised, sprained or broken her ankle. 'It looks like a sprained ankle to me, darling. But let's put it in cold water to take down the swelling and before school I'll take you to the doctor.'

'Why can't you doctor it, Mummy?' Lucy Jane asked, as Mrs Tadworth was a doctor herself, and had a clinic two afternoons a week at the local hospital.

15

'Because, darling, it's always best to use an outside doctor for the family, not the mother or father,' her mother said, collecting a bowl and putting ice and water in it.

Lucy Jane squealed as her mother pushed her foot into the bowl of icy cold water. 'Oh, this is horrid,' she said as the water covered her foot. Then she looked up and suddenly exclaimed, 'Dancing frogs!' She had noticed the drips of rain on the window pane.

As she tried to twiddle her toes in the icy cold water she wondered what the doctor would say, and if she had broken her foot or toes or worse still her ankle? Maybe she would never be able to dance again, maybe she'd have to use crutches and would hobble like a very

old lady for the rest of her life. 'I'm only ten,' she thought. 'I'm too young not to be able to walk. Too young.' The drama in Lucy Jane's head grew greater by the minute.

'Come on, Lucy, breakfast,' her mother said. 'Quickly. I've rung the doctor and he's expecting us any minute.'

'But what about my exam?' Lucy Jane said, now very worried.

'We'll see about your exam,' her mother answered, 'when we know what's the matter with your foot.'

After breakfast Lucy Jane, plus ballet clothes, Jeremy and Mr Tadworth, bundled into Mrs Tadworth's little red car and drove off to the doctor.

'We'll drop you off at Richmond station, darling,' Mrs Tadworth said to her husband as she started the car. When Mr Tadworth left the car to go to work Lucy Jane took Jeremy's hand and gave it a little squeeze. 'I may have broken my foot, Jem Jem,' Lucy Jane whispered. 'That's why we're going to the doctor.'

When they arrived at the doctor's and were sitting in his neat little green and white surgery, the doctor took Lucy Jane's foot in his hand and gently pushed and pulled it in different directions.

'Well,' the doctor said after a long pause. 'A ballet exam today, eh? Well what can I tell you?'

'Tell me I can dance today and that nothing is wrong with my foot,' Lucy Jane pleaded immediately. 'Or how I can get it better,' she added.

The doctor shook his head. 'I don't like to upset you, but I don't think you can dance today.'

17

'*What?*' Lucy Jane exclaimed and jumped to her feet. 'Ouch,' she said and immediately fell back into her chair again.

'I'll strap the ankle up today and you can go to school but don't play games, and you can possibly dance tomorrow or the day after,' he said as he took a bandage from the cupboard and wrapped it round Lucy Jane's bad foot.

A terrible sinking feeling filled Lucy Jane's heart and a sensation of despair swam through her head. 'No, no, no,' she kept saying to herself. 'It's not true. I have to dance today. I have to take the exam. I have to *pass.*'

Mrs Tadworth put her arm round Lucy Jane's shoulders and Jeremy squeezed Lucy Jane's knee. 'Don't cry, 'Ucy,' he said. ''Ucy big girl. Don't cry.'

Lucy Jane smiled sadly at her brother.

'I've got some Arnica and Rusta grav cream at the house,' Mrs Tadworth suddenly suggested. 'Perhaps that would be a good idea?'

'Yes, excellent,' the doctor said. 'Arnica's a herb cream, Lucy Jane, made from the arnica flower that grows in alpine meadows, and it's been used for healing for thousands of years. I'm sure it will do your foot a lot of good.'

'Why can't I have something new?' Lucy Jane appealed to the doctor. 'Haven't you anything modern to get me better?'

'Don't be silly, Lucy,' her mother said. 'We've used arnica lots of times to stop you getting a bruise when you've fallen down,' Mrs Tadworth said as they rose to leave the surgery.

After Mrs Tadworth had taken Lucy Jane home to get the arnica cream, she decided that it would be best to take her daughter straight to school, swollen foot and ballet clothes and all.

But the big question in Lucy Jane's mind was what would she do if she couldn't do her exam today, and how could she arrange for her exam to be postponed until her foot was better?

'I must see Miss Sweetfoot,' Lucy Jane said as she arrived at school. 'I must see if I can change the exam.' And she hobbled out of the car to see Mrs Pierce, the headmistress, to ask if she could see Miss Sweetfoot. But Mrs Pierce wasn't there. Lucy Jane became very agitated when the secretary said, 'Miss Sweetfoot is busy all morning preparing everything for the exams. She can't see you today.'

'But she must,' Lucy Jane answered without thinking how rude this must sound. 'I must see her to ask if I can take my ballet exam another day. I've hurt my foot.'

The secretary, Sylvia Sloane, peered down at Lucy Jane. 'I'll see what I can do,' she said and showed Lucy Jane the door. Lucy Jane decided that she would go and find Miss Sweetfoot herself even if she had to wait until break-time.

At break-time Lucy Jane, with her best friends Julie and Jasmine, went to search for her ballet teacher. The three girls ran, skipped and hobbled along the corridor as fast as they could to find Miss Sweetfoot. Finally they found Miss Sweetfoot in the gymnasium sorting out the exam papers ready for the examination that afternoon. She looked up.

'Girls, what on earth are you doing here? Your exam isn't until after lunch and your exam, Jasmine, is not until . . .' Miss Sweetfoot didn't manage to finish as all three girls interrupted, 'Miss Sweetfoot, we . . .'

'Now, now, one at a time,' Miss Sweetfoot said looking at the girls in turn. 'What is it?'

'Miss Sweetfoot, Lucy Jane has hurt herself and can't dance today,' Jasmine said giving Lucy Jane a sympathetic hug. Miss Sweetfoot looked extremely concerned. 'Oh dear, this is bad news. No exam, no competition. Oh dear,' she said again.

'No competition!' Lucy Jane exclaimed feeling quite faint at the thought of missing the Golden Star competition.

Suddenly Miss Sweetfoot stood up with a smile. 'I know,' she said. 'Jasmine and Lucy Jane can change places. Jasmine can you do her exam today and let Lucy Jane take your place the day after tomorrow?'

Lucy Jane smiled with relief and Jasmine nodded happily, pleased that she was able to help her friend.

'You can borrow my clothes, Jasmine,' Lucy Jane said trying to help.

'Good,' Jasmine replied. In fact, Jasmine was happy to get her exam over and not have to wait two days.

'But,' Miss Sweetfoot continued, 'if you want to dance in two days, Lucy, you'd better go home, put your foot in ice cold water and keep it there as long as you can. I'll speak to Mrs Pierce about the change of plan straight away,' and she walked briskly out of the room whistling a little music from one of the ballet exercises.

So it was settled far more simply than any of the girls

21

could have imagined and, provided Lucy Jane rested her foot and it got better in two days, for the time being the 'big drama' was over.

3

The Exam

Lucy Jane was relieved that in the next two days the swelling on her foot went down little by little. 'I don't think I need a bandage any more. The Rusta grav and the Arnica cream and icy water must have done the trick,' she said to herself.

Now she had to see if she could walk or, more importantly, dance. In her pretty peach and white bedroom, Lucy Jane tried out one or two steps, and although it was a little painful at times she felt that her foot was almost back to normal, and was strong enough for her to take her exam that afternoon.

That afternoon. Suddenly Lucy Jane felt very nervous. What if her foot failed her? The thought filled her with terror. 'Please don't let me fall or do anything silly or not know my theory or forget the steps of the *enchaînement*,' she prayed quietly to herself. She had worked so hard for this exam, done so much practice, she couldn't bear to fail now.

At school that afternoon, as Lucy Jane changed into her pink tights, leotard, and pink satin ballet shoes

ready for the exam, she felt a mixture of excitement and fear, she wondered if the examiner would think she was Jasmine as she had changed places with her. She carefully tied the satin ribbons of her new ballet shoes round her sore ankle and did a neat bow at the back so that the ends wouldn't show and hoped that her foot would not let her down.

Margaret Barry, a tall slim pretty girl and the first girl to be examined that afternoon, flew out of the room after the exam and threw herself into Miss Sweetfoot's arms saying, 'It was awful. Nothing was the same as in the class and I couldn't even remember what *pas de chat* meant.'

'Really, Margaret,' Miss Sweetfoot said shaking her head. 'I hope if any of you other girls are asked, you'll say it means . . .' and she waited for someone to reply as she patted Margaret on the shoulder.

'The step of the cat,' Lucy Jane said quickly and Tanya James added, 'Like this,' and she did a neat little *pas de chat*.

Tanya was the next girl on the list and she looked very confident as she strode into the room. As Lucy Jane waited, it seemed as if Tanya was in the exam for ever. Lucy Jane wished she hadn't got ready so early because the waiting made her feel so nervous.

Miss Sweetfoot came over to her, looked down kindly, put her hand on her cheek and said, 'Cheer up, Lucy. I know you'll do well. You must believe in yourself. You must go in with your head up, shoulders back and a smile. I haven't told you this before, but you are one of the best girls in the class. Of the thirty girls from the school, who are taking ballet exams this term, you are one of my big hopes.'

Lucy Jane could hardly believe what she was hearing. 'Me?' she asked, amazed.

'Yes, *you*,' Miss Sweetfoot said, laughing.

Now Lucy Jane felt she really had to do well. If Miss Sweetfoot thought she was good, she couldn't let her down. Suddenly, the words 'Next girl' went shooting through Lucy Jane's ears and she knew that, finally, it was *her* turn. The butterflies in her tummy, the frogs in her head, jelly in her legs all started fluttering, jumping and wobbling all at once.

'Come on, foot, don't let me down,' she said to herself and took a deep breath and walked boldly into the room, pretending she was not afraid.

At the end of the room there was a long trestle table with a green baize cloth over it and a jug of water and glass set to one side. In the chair behind the table sat a rather cross-looking lady, a little older than Lucy Jane's mother, wearing horn-rimmed spectacles and very red lipstick. Her shiny black hair was pulled back into a knot on the top of her head which made her long neck look even longer. She peered over her glasses and spoke in a soft drawling voice, 'Now, you're Jasmine – I mean Lucy Jane. You've hurt your foot, I hear.'

There was a pause and at last Lucy Jane said, 'Yes, but I hope it's well enough to dance now.'

'So do I,' the examiner said slowly, 'otherwise we're all wasting our time, aren't we?' She finished slowly and gave Lucy Jane a sickly smile. Lucy Jane was rather surprised. She had never thought of a dancing exam as a waste of time. Then the examiner suddenly commanded, 'Take off your glasses, dear.'

Lucy Jane had completely forgotten that she still had her glasses on so she quickly took them off and put them on the edge of the examiner's table.

'What's *your* name?' Lucy Jane suddenly asked.

'Nicolette Dalton,' the examiner replied, surprised at being asked. 'Now come on, dear, let's begin.'

Although this was not the first ballet exam Lucy Jane had taken, she was suddenly very aware of being all alone in the room. At that moment she longed to have a friend to look at to check she was doing the right thing.

But luckily there was the familiar sight of Miss Harp, the pianist, smiling at her from the piano and

giving her an encouraging nod. Lucy Jane walked swiftly back to the *barre* and stood with her shoulders back, her feet in first position with her knees well pulled up and her ballet exam began.

For the first minutes as Lucy Jane did her *battements tendues* and *pliés* it was hard to concentrate or hear the music or the examiner properly, and she found herself frowning and biting her lip a lot as she worked her way through her *barre* exercises. Her hand became very hot and slipped as it gripped the wooden bar. But when

she was in the centre of the room and she had to do the *enchaînements* Lucy Jane remembered all the steps she was told to put together perfectly, and suddenly she found she was dancing easily and enjoying the music and expressing herself through her arms and the steps with great charm and musicality. It was a happy feeling which made Lucy Jane's head feel light and her heart full, especially while she did the set exercises she had practised so often at home.

When she had finished and the pianist had played the last chord on the piano she heard the examiner murmur, 'Mmmm, mmmm,' to herself. Lucy Jane wasn't sure if this was good or bad but she hoped it meant that Nicolette Dalton liked the way she had danced.

However, the great thing was Lucy Jane had completely forgotten about her foot. It seemed as if it hadn't hurt her at all, and she had managed to finish the exam without falling down or doing any of the things she'd dreaded.

4

Waiting

Because of the generous way in which Jasmine had let Lucy Jane change places with her, Lucy Jane and Jasmine's friendship grew even closer and it was almost as though they had become sisters.

One day they were all looking at the notice board with Julie, who was Lucy Jane's oldest friend. Suddenly Jasmine said in a hushed tone, 'This sounds exciting.' And she read the announcement on the board.

> All girls wishing to improve their dancing and their chances in local or national dancing festivals are invited to take a two-week dancing course (tap, ballet, modern and jazz included) at the Belle Adroit Summer Dancing Camp in Cornwall. Details available from your headmistress.

'That sounds wonderful. Do you think we could all go?' Jasmine said excitedly.

'It'll certainly help us improve,' Julie added, not

really keen on the idea of going to a dancing summer camp.

'*And* if we can all go we'll all be together,' Lucy Jane finished enthusiastically. 'It would be wonderful.' The girls all seemed delighted at the idea and couldn't wait to ask their parents that night.

'Summer camp sounds so grown-up,' Jasmine said as they collected their things at the end of the day.

At home that evening Lucy Jane wasn't too sure how to bring up the subject of the camp. She felt sure her parents would want her to visit her granny in Scotland again this summer. But she had to try so she said, 'Julie's and Jasmine's mummies may be sending them to summer dancing camp in August to help them to do better in the Golden Star Dancing Festival.' There was a pause, then Lucy Jane added, 'I'd like to go too, Mummy, if you'll let me.'

'Let's wait until we know your exam results,' her mother said, as she continued to wash the dishes. 'But it may be too expensive.'

Lucy Jane was upset that her mother hadn't said yes straight away, but at least her mother's reply wasn't a definite no. But Lucy Jane knew that if she didn't pass her exam it would surely be no and that would be the end of her chance of going to the summer camp, and of being in the competition.

During the following weeks all the girls waited patiently for the exam results, and Lucy Jane had to put the idea of going to camp out of her mind for the time being. She still worked hard preparing for the dancing festival in case she qualified to enter the ballet

31

section. The thought of dancing in front of four judges, who were famous ballet stars, really appealed to her. She could imagine herself floating and turning to the music on the stage at the Albert Hall in a beautiful ballet dress and wearing make-up. Might she even win a prize?

Lucy Jane loved to dance more than anything in the world. She had been in a television film last summer holidays, and even won an award for her role, but nothing had been as wonderful as appearing on stage at Covent Garden in the *Nutcracker* two Christmases before, when her mother had been in hospital having Jeremy.

One break-time Lucy Jane and Jasmine were walking together along the corridor talking about the exam when they bumped into Miss Sweetfoot, who said, 'I think you should do an extra ballet class each week, Jasmine. It'll help your tap.'

Jasmine was delighted, as although she preferred tap to ballet, this meant she could spend more time with Lucy Jane.

So at the next ballet class the girls arrived at the class together but, to everyone's amazement, Lucy Jane was wearing tap shoes, black tights and a bright red leotard instead of pink tights, pink shoes and a white ballet tunic, and Jasmine was wearing her normal ballet clothes.

Miss Sweetfoot walked straight over to Lucy Jane. She looked down at her amazed.

'Have you forgotten which class it is?' Miss Sweetfoot asked Lucy Jane.

Lucy Jane didn't answer and instead she did a few

bright tap steps, a couple of turns and stopped with her arm outstretched as though waiting for applause. Then she started to giggle.

'What on earth has come over you?' Miss Sweetfoot said, trying not to giggle herself. 'It is so unlike you, Lucy Jane, to play the fool during your dancing class.' Miss Sweetfoot continued, 'Come on, Lucy, you'd better get changed.'

Lucy Jane stopped giggling and smiled at Miss Sweetfoot, anxious to say something that had been troubling her for some time. But she couldn't speak and there was a long pause.

'Come on, Lucy. What's the matter?'

'What will happen if I don't pass the ballet exam?' Lucy Jane asked suddenly, her voice close to tears.

'But you will pass,' Jasmine piped in. 'I keep telling you it's silly to worry. You're the best.'

Lucy Jane didn't answer and she waited to see what Miss Sweetfoot thought.

Suddenly Miss Sweetfoot threw her arms in the air and exclaimed, 'I don't believe this. I wouldn't put you girls into the exam if I thought you were going to fail. Now come on, get ready for the class at once, Lucy,' and she gave Lucy Jane a little tap on the cheek, then pushed her in the direction of the changing-room, still smiling and shaking her head, surprised that Lucy Jane had been so worried about the exam.

Then she clapped her hands and all the girls rushed to the *barre* to start their exercises.

Some weeks later at school assembly Mrs Pierce, the headmistress, made an announcement. 'The results of the music exams, ballet exams and national dancing exams have come through and rather than read them all out now, I would like those girls concerned to go to the gymnasium before lunch to collect their results.' Mrs Pierce adjusted the jacket of her green suit and walked from the room. Lucy Jane, Jasmine and Julie grabbed hands in anticipation. But before the girls had time to say a word the bell went for the first lesson and they all shuffled out of the hall.

'Well,' Tanya said as they arrived at the door of the classroom, 'I'm bound to have got honours, but I doubt if you'll even pass, Lucy Jane. What a fool you were to take the exam with a wonky ankle,' and she swept on past the three girls with a superior smile on her face.

'Take no notice of her nonsense,' Jasmine said comfortingly. 'I'm surprised she didn't say to me, "I doubt if you'll pass as you're black",' she added indignantly.

'But Jasmine, everyone knows that you have the best *grands jetés* in the class,' Julie said.

'And you do the best tap, splits, arabesques and back bends,' Lucy Jane added loyally as they hurried to their desks.

'*Venez, mes enfants,*' Mademoiselle Claudine, the French teacher, called. '*If faut commencer la classe.*' So everyone sat down to start the French lesson.

Although Lucy Jane tried to work hard she was longing for the morning to end. By the time it was 12.45 she had convinced herself that she hadn't passed the exam and by the look of Julie's and Jasmine's faces, they felt the same, too.

'I feel sick,' Julie said as the girls walked to the gymnasium.

'So do I,' Jasmine and Lucy Jane agreed. When all the girls had arrived Mrs Pierce announced, 'There is an envelope for each of the girls who took the exam. Please come up and collect your results as I call out your names in alphabetical order.'

'Tadworth T,' Lucy Jane thought, 'I'll be one of the last.'

Tanya Avon was one of the first girls to go up. She strode up to Mrs Pierce smiling and as she opened her envelope left with a grim look on her face. 'I've done frightfully well,' she said to Lucy Jane when she returned to her place. 'Won't tell you how well as it'll make you jealous.'

Lucy Jane looked at her, doubting she was telling the truth. Jasmine and Julie were called next. But they didn't dare open their envelopes straight away. 'Let's wait until you've got yours, Lucy.' So the three girls waited together, butterflies in their stomachs, until at last Lucy Jane's name was called. Heart beating fast, ears pink with excitement, her frog hopping in her head, she ran up to collect her results. When the three girls were together they took a deep breath before they opened their envelopes.

'What if we've failed?' Lucy Jane said nervously.

'Let's be brave and look at the results together,' Julie said.

Lucy Jane, cheeks pink, adjusted her glasses and nodded.

'Well,' Jasmine said, 'shall we all say it together?'

'Right,' Lucy Jane said. 'One, two, three,' and all the three girls called out, 'Failed,' and burst out laughing, falling over each other and waving their arms with their envelopes above their heads.

'No, seriously,' Jasmine said trying not to laugh, 'let's start again. One, two, three.'

'HONOURS,' the three girls shouted out together and skipped and danced and hugged each other as though this was the happiest day of their lives.

'We all qualify for the Golden Star,' Lucy Jane said ecstatically. 'We've passed. Hurray! Isn't it wonderful?'

As they were about to leave they looked down on to the floor and noticed that one of the girls had dropped their exam results. Lucy Jane picked it up and noticed that it was Tanya's. She didn't dare look at the results, but at that moment Miss Sweetfoot came up and asked, 'Happy, girls?'

'Someone dropped this,' Lucy Jane said offering Miss Sweetfoot the piece of paper. Miss Sweetfoot took the exam result and shook her head as she thanked Lucy Jane.

'Oh dear,' she said as she walked away. 'Tanya, my only failure.' And she turned out of the gymnasium making her usual little whistle.

When they left school that night three happier girls it would have been hard to find.

The following day they waited to hear if Miss Sweetfoot would definitely let them enter the Golden Star Dancing Festival. Then if she did, they had to see if their parents would let them go to the summer camp. If they could just achieve this the rest of the year was going to be very exciting for them.

5

The Decision

When Lucy Jane's parents saw her exam results they were extremely proud.

'Does this mean you'll definitely take part in the Golden Star Dancing Festival?' Lucy Jane's mother asked as she hugged her daughter.

'The problem is,' Lucy Jane replied seriously, 'I don't really know. I hope so. Miss Sweetfoot is telling us tomorrow. You see, we can't all enter, only a certain number from each school.' Lucy Jane looked down at the results in her mother's hand and ran her finger over the word honours.

'I see,' her mother replied thoughtfully. 'Then we'll have to hope for the best.'

Lucy Jane nodded.

'Will you let me go to the summer dancing camp if I do get into the competition?' Lucy Jane asked anxiously.

'Probably, darling, but I'll have to ask Daddy and it depends on how much it costs.'

Lucy felt a little disappointed that her mother still

hadn't said a definite yes. But there was nothing she could do and no more was said on the subject that evening. So Lucy Jane settled back to enjoy her favourite television programme, *The Cosby Show*, before she went to bed.

Three days passed and there was no mention at school about the dancing festival. The following Wednesday at the ballet class Lucy Jane could contain her curiosity no longer and she had to ask, 'Miss Sweetfoot, are we going to be allowed to enter the Golden Star competition?'

'Ah,' Miss Sweetfoot said slowly, 'I was coming to that. Now, those girls who still want to enter the festival please remain behind at the end of the class and I will explain all the details to them, and discuss how many of you will be able to enter.'

Lucy Jane jumped up and down with excitement and Tanya looked at her in disgust.

'I'd *hate* to be in a dancing festival,' Tanya said. 'I can think of nothing worse. It would ruin my holiday in the south of France if I had to practise all the time.' And she flounced from the room without so much as an 'excuse me' to Miss Sweetfoot.

Julie, Jasmine and Lucy Jane looked at each other in surprise.

'I'm desperate to be in the festival,' Lucy Jane admitted.

'So am I,' Jasmine agreed and half of the rest of the class joined in too.

At the end of the lesson Miss Sweetfoot said, 'This is what I think should happen. Three girls should enter the ballet section, three the modern section and three the Scottish dancing. That way the best girls in each group can enter.'

The girls all looked at each other wondering for which group they'd be chosen. Lucy Jane didn't really want to do Scottish and hoped she wouldn't have to.

Jasmine didn't really want to do ballet and Julie had suddenly decided that she didn't want to enter the festival, as she wanted to go on a horse-riding holiday with her cousin in the summer holidays so didn't want to go to the dancing camp at all.

Finally Miss Sweetfoot said, 'Jane, Jasmine and Sally I'd like you all to do modern.'

'Hurray,' Jasmine cried out, delighted to be doing tap and modern instead of ballet.

'Julie, Simone and Lucy Jane should do ballet. And Naomi, Sandra and Diane should take Scottish.'

There was a silence in the room. No one spoke until Lucy Jane suddenly said, 'Jumping cactus, *ballet* is just what I wanted.' Then the other girls joined in with their comments, while Miss Sweetfoot wrote down the names of those who wanted to enter and those who did not.

Lucy Jane left the ballet class extremely happy that night. She was going to dance a solo in a real ballet dress at the Albert Hall. It would be a dream come true.

But the next big hurdle was to see if Lucy Jane and Jasmine could persuade their parents to let them go to camp. This turned out to be a bigger hurdle than the girls had expected and almost as difficult as passing the ballet exam – worse, really, because that was up to them, going away depended on their parents.

'It's no good, Lucy. The summer dance camp is just too expensive. It just isn't possible to find the money at the moment,' Mrs Tadworth said to Lucy Jane over lunch. 'Don't ask me again, because the answer will be no.'

Lucy Jane's hopes were dashed.

Then, after lunch, while they were all walking by the river, suddenly an idea came to her. 'I know. I'll ask Granny to help. Maybe she can persuade Mummy to use the money I got from the film I made in Scotland last year to pay for the camp.'

So that night, when her mother was putting Jeremy

to bed and her father was working in his study, Lucy Jane crept into the sitting-room to telephone her grandmother. But to her dismay she discovered her granny wasn't at home. So Lucy Jane decided she would try again when her parents were having their supper. Nine o'clock came, and Lucy Jane should have been asleep, but she was still awake waiting for her parents to go into the sitting-room. On Sunday nights they usually ate their supper there on a tray and Lucy Jane knew that when the door was closed it would be safe to phone.

Click. 'That's it,' Lucy Jane thought as she heard the door close. 'They've settled in.' And she dashed to her parents' bedroom to use the phone.

'Oh, rabbits,' she said suddenly. 'Now I can't remember the number.' She was so nervous and excited she even forgot her glasses. This made her feel really silly as earlier she had dialled the number perfectly correctly. She would have to creep downstairs and look up the number in the address book on the hall table. If she was caught her secret would be discovered. But she had to risk it, otherwise her only chance of going to the camp was gone.

Halfway down the stairs she heard her mother say, 'I'll just go and fetch the mustard, darling,' and then she heard the sitting-room door open and her mother go into the kitchen. Lucy Jane flattened herself against the wall, hoping her mother wouldn't hear her or see her. She waited trembling until she heard the sitting-room door close again. Then Lucy Jane made her way to the hall to look for the address book on the hall table.

'Rats,' she said. 'I've left my glasses upstairs.' So she took the book upstairs to her parents' bedroom where she tried to dial again. This time her granny was at home.

'Hello, dearie,' she heard her granny's sweet surprised voice say. 'What are you doing up so late?'

'It's a secret, Granny. I want to go to summer dancing camp and we haven't got the money. Can you help me? Please persuade Mummy to let me use the money they gave me for making *The Russell Adventure.*'

'Well, dearie, this all comes as a bit of a shock. Why isn't Mummy asking me? Let me think about it overnight. Now you go back to bed, and I'll telephone you tomorrow evening.'

'But, Granny, you will try to do something, won't you? It's *terribly* important,' Lucy Jane said. Then she kissed her granny goodnight over the phone and crept back to bed.

She lay in bed wondering if her mother had heard her or noticed that someone had used the telephone or moved the address book. Suddenly she leapt out of bed.

'Jumping cactus,' she squealed. 'I left the address book on Mummy's bed,' and she hurried into the bedroom to straighten the bedcovers and take the address book downstairs.

Halfway down she heard the sitting-room door open again. 'Is that you, Lucy?' her mother called up the stairs. Lucy Jane didn't dare answer. She had made a stupid mistake and now she was going to be caught.

When she heard the door close again she flew down

the stairs with the address book, taking care not to fall on the last step again. She carefully put the book on the hall table, then tapped on the sitting-room door and said, 'Mummy, I can't sleep. I keep thinking about the camp.'

Her mother put down her tray and came over to her. 'Sweetheart,' she said, 'nothing will be resolved by lying awake. Go to sleep and who knows . . .?' She didn't finish her sentence. Then she added, 'Who knows . . .' again and gave Lucy Jane a kiss.

Lucy Jane kissed her mother and father goodnight and obediently went back upstairs to bed.

The next evening after school Lucy Jane waited anxiously for the telephone to ring. Suddenly it did and it gave her a terrible fright, too.

'I'll get it, I'll get it,' she cried, rushing to the telephone, the pot of marmite still in her hand. She wanted to get there before her mother.

'Hello,' she said breathlessly. 'Is that you . . .? Oh, Mrs Cartwright, do you want to speak to Mummy?' she continued, disappointed, and handed the receiver to her mother. Her mother and Mrs Cartwright seemed to talk for ever which meant Granny would wonder what was wrong if she couldn't get through. 'I hope she'll keep trying,' Lucy Jane said to herself, biting her lip anxiously.

But up in Scotland her grandmother had completely forgotten about her promise to Lucy Jane and was enjoying her afternoon tea. It was only when Mrs Tamm, the housekeeper, asked, while clearing the tea tray, 'How's our wee Lucy in London, Mrs Mackenzie?' that her grandmother remembered.

45

'Lucy? Oh, Tammy, I'd completely forgotten! I said I would telephone her tonight as she wants me to persuade her mother to let her go to summer dancing camp.'

'Och, if I know Lucy, she'll manage to go whether you persuade her mother or not. So you may as well persuade her,' Mrs Tamm said as she turned smiling into the kitchen holding the tray.

Mrs Mackenzie thought Mrs Tamm was right. Lucy was so determined and practical, she usually got her way. She was very fond of little Lucy and it always made her happy when Lucy was happy, so she decided she would help her granddaughter and telephoned London, but the line was busy.

'Engaged. Ah, well, I'll try later,' Mrs Mackenzie said.

Back in London Lucy Jane was getting more and more worried. Why hadn't her grandmother telephoned? Finally, Lucy Jane said to her mother, 'Why don't we telephone Granny?'

At that moment the telephone rang again, and Lucy Jane rushed over to answer it. It was Mrs Cartwright again. 'Lucy, I forgot to tell your mother that I've got tickets for the puppet show on *Saturday* afternoon and not *Friday* after school as I had said.'

'I'll tell her,' Lucy Jane said as politely as she could and quickly replaced the receiver. 'Now can we ring Granny?' Lucy Jane started again, and no sooner had she said 'Granny' than the telephone rang once more. 'I expect it's Mrs Cartwright again,' Lucy Jane said gloomily and picked up the receiver. 'Granny. Oh, Granny, it's you.' The relief in Lucy Jane's heart was

complete. Granny hadn't forgotten her.

'Can I speak to your mother, dearie?' her grandmother said and Lucy Jane obediently handed over the phone to her mother, praying that Granny had good news.

It seemed to Lucy Jane that her mother and Granny were chatting about everything under the sun except the summer camp. Then she heard, 'Well, if you really think so, Mother.' 'Then I suppose there can't be any harm. But she seems a little young to me to be away from home and it's so expensive.' There was a long pause. Lucy Jane's heart was beating like a drum.

'Well, I suppose we could,' her mother continued. 'Yes. Yes, I'll speak to her father tonight. Goodbye, Mother,' and Mrs Tadworth replaced the receiver and walked straight over to Lucy Jane with a questioning look on her face.

'So, who's been ringing Granny in the middle of the night?' Lucy Jane's mother asked with a broad grin. 'Who's a determined, mischievous, devious little monkey?' She took her daughter and shook her warmly. Before Lucy Jane could answer her mother said, 'YES I think you can go to the summer camp, but only if your father says yes too.'

This was all in the world that Lucy Jane had wanted to hear. She was so happy she hugged her mother. Now if her father said yes, and she felt sure he would, she had a chance to improve her dancing and perhaps had the chance of winning a prize in the Golden Star Festival, too.

'Oh, Mummy, you are so sweet and kind to me,' Lucy Jane said, hugging her mother again. 'I'm so happy, I can't wait to tell Jasmine that I shall probably be going with her after all. I'll write to Granny and thank her for persuading you.'

When Mr Tadworth returned from work Lucy Jane waited anxiously upstairs in her room while her mother and father discussed the summer camp. It seemed much later when she had already finished writing to her grandmother that her father came upstairs and stood in the doorway. 'So I hear you have already persuaded your mother and Granny to let you go to the

48

Belle Adroit Summer Camp. Now I suppose it's just up to me to agree,' he paused, 'or not,' he said smiling, rather enjoying keeping Lucy Jane in suspense. The look of fear on poor little Lucy Jane's face made Mr Tadworth smile even more.

'I think I need another twenty-four hours to think about this,' he said, his eyes twinkling with mischief.

'Oh no,' Lucy Jane pleaded. 'I thought it was all settled. I've written to thank Granny,' she added.

After a moment her father picked up the letter lying on the bedside table. He read it silently and then looked at his daughter.

'This is a very nice, well-written letter,' he said impressed. 'It looks to me from this letter that you are definitely expecting to go to summer camp.' Then he took Lucy Jane's hand and said kindly, 'Any girl who writes such a sweet and thoughtful letter as this deserves to go to camp,' and he picked Lucy Jane up and gave her a hug.

'My word, you'll soon be too big to put on my knee,' her father remarked.

Again the joy of knowing she was really going to the camp filled her whole body right from the hairs on top of her head down to her fingertips. She kissed her father and thanked him. Now she had something very special to look forward to.

6

Old Friends

On 1 August the great day came. Lucy Jane had hardly slept the night before she was so excited.

When Lucy Jane and Jasmine arrived at the summer camp they were greeted by two smiling women dressed in jeans and T-shirts with the name of the camp written across the front. The ladies welcomed the girls with a firm handshake.

'Now you're safely here, go over to the dining-hall, get a glass of orange juice and some fruit. Then at 5.30 we'll meet beneath the big oak tree near the gates to the camp. We'll give out the timetables, so you'll know where and when your classes and the activities are to be held.' The two ladies smiled at the girls and Lucy Jane and Jasmine nodded happily and rushed off to join the other children in the dining-hall.

'I wonder who else will be sharing our room,' Jasmine asked nervously as she took Lucy Jane's hand. They both felt a little apprehensive. Lucy Jane had been away from home by herself before but that was staying with her granny.

The hall was a long wooden hut, the inside of which was rather like a church hall, very plain with a wooden floor. It was extremely noisy as there was an echo, and every time anyone moved their chair, put down a cup or laughed it echoed and made a tremendous racket which was hard on the ears and made it difficult to hear and think.

As the girls queued up for their orange juice, Lucy Jane suddenly stopped in her tracks. 'Move along, orange pips,' a familiar voice said cheekily.

Lucy Jane spun round. 'Angela!' she exclaimed. There was Angela, her friend from Scotland whom she hadn't seen since last winter.

'Jumping cactus, Ange,' Lucy Jane exclaimed excitedly. 'I don't believe it! You're here too,' and she gave Angela a hug. 'This is Jasmine, my friend from school,' she proudly pushed Jasmine towards Angela. 'She's a fantastic dancer and does the best splits and back bends in the school.'

'Nice to meet you, black eyes,' Angela said happily and held out her hand. Jasmine laughed and took Angela's hand warmly.

'So you've grown your hair, Ange,' Lucy Jane commented seeing that Angela's hair was now very neat and shoulder length.

'Yes, Mr Savage is keeping an eye on me. Won't let me cut me hair again,' she said with a twinkle. Lucy Jane always enjoyed Angela's way of speaking. 'He's paid for me to come here to improve me Scottish dancing for the next film. I'll be quite a toff when he's finished with me,' Angela laughed.

Angela and Lucy Jane had met, became rivals, and

51

then best friends the previous summer when Lucy Jane had gone to stay with her granny in Scotland. Both Angela and Lucy Jane had wanted to be in the film, *The Russell Adventure*, but Angela had got the part. However, in the end, Angela had cut her hair off as she hadn't really wanted to be in the film, so Lucy Jane had played the role of Isabella instead.*

Now they were firm friends and Mr Savage had Angela under contract and was grooming her to star in his next film. Lucy Jane had loved being in the film, but ballet was her real love, and even though she had won a BAFTA* award for the 'Best Newcomer' she knew that acting was not for her. Ballet made her feel really happy and in the words of Miss Sweetfoot made her 'spirits soar'.

'Who would have thought you would be here?' Lucy Jane exclaimed happily. 'Tell me, what room are you in?' Lucy Jane asked hoping that Angela might be sharing a room with her and Jasmine.

'Oh, I think I'm in number . . .' She paused searching in her pockets for the number. 'Oh, fiddlesticks, I've lost me bit of paper telling me which number. But I hope we are.'

After all the children had their orange juice they assembled by the big oak tree waiting for their instructions for the following day. There were boys and girls of all ages from ten to fourteen. The boys from the tennis sports camp next door were carrying tennis rackets or cricket bats and were dressed in track suits, running shorts or tennis whites. The girls from

* See *Lucy Jane on Television*
* British Association of Film and Television Arts

52

the dancing camp were all rather slim with their hair pulled back from their faces and tied in a pony tail or a bun and wearing tight jeans and large floppy T-shirts.

As Lucy Jane stood next to her friends she suddenly felt rather apprehensive. What would be expected of her? Would she be able to keep up? She linked arms with Angela and Jasmine and said anxiously, 'Good luck, everyone.' At that moment Sarah Smith announced, 'I have here a copy of the timetable for each girl and boy. After you have collected the timetable with your name on, will you go to your cabin and unpack your suitcases which will be waiting outside? Then girls please come back to the girls' dining-hall by 6.30 for an early supper, and the boys to the boys' camp dining-hall. At 8.30 tomorrow after breakfast, you'll be shown round the camp. And remember the boys and girls are in *separate* camps but you will occasionally have to use the same facilities, such as the swimming pool. But this, I'm happy to tell you, will not be at the same time!' All the children laughed and then Miss Smith added, 'Good luck, work hard and have a happy stay.' With that Sarah Smith gave a wave and made her way towards the main house.

Lucy Jane was sad they weren't going to see the boys again. When the girls arrived at their chalet, their luggage was already waiting for them on the steps. Lucy Jane quickly looked to see if Angela's luggage was there too, but it wasn't.

All the chalets were joined together and were like a long row of beach huts, made of wood, painted blue and marked 'Students' or 'Staff'.

Angela came rushing up to Lucy Jane. 'Plenty of teachers' cabins, I see. No midnight feasts or high jinks with all those watchdogs around,' she said jauntily and sauntered off again. The idea of midnight feasts thrilled Lucy Jane. She hoped they'd manage one.

Lucy Jane and Jasmine were still standing by the suitcases on the chalet's little porch when Lucy Jane said, 'Come on, better get unpacked,' and pulling herself together she heaved the two girls' suitcases into the chalet.

As they entered the room they were surprised to see a rather shy girl of about eleven already sitting on one of the beds.

'I'm sorry. I've already chosen a bed, as it was the nearest to the door.'

'That's all right,' Lucy Jane said brightly. Then she noticed as the girl stood up and walked across the dormitory that she had a slight limp. The girl immediately sat down in the nearest chair.

'I'm Lucy Jane. This is my friend Jasmine. Her parents are in the government in Barbados and she goes to my school. What's your name?'

'Mary Ellen,' the girl with the limp replied. 'I'm doing national dancing. You know, country dancing, but mainly Scottish. What are you doing?'

Lucy Jane studied the pretty fair-haired girl sitting rather tiredly in the chair and said, 'I'm doing ballet, and Jasmine's doing modern tap. We're both hoping to be in the Golden Star Dancing Festival.'

'Oh, so am I,' Mary Ellen replied and jumped up enthusiastically before moving unsteadily across to her bed.

'Have you hurt your foot?' Lucy Jane asked Mary Ellen as she flopped back on to the pillow.

'No, not really. I was born with one leg shorter than the other so I have a slight limp, especially when I'm tired. But it doesn't seem to affect my dancing,' she laughed. 'The doctors say it's because I like dancing so much.'

'Oh, yes,' Jasmine and Lucy Jane joined in. 'So do we.'

Mary Ellen had learnt every trick imaginable to disguise the fact that one leg was not as strong as the other, and that the heel of her right foot didn't touch the ground. This didn't matter when she was doing Scottish dancing, as she was always on the balls of her feet, but for everyday life she had to have the heel of her right shoe built up, or special pads put under the heel inside her trainers to make both legs appear the same.

'Who's sleeping on the fourth bed?' Lucy Jane suddenly asked, as she looked round the little white room, with its one window at the back and two small windows at the front. It had four beds, four small chests of drawers and two little cupboards for hanging their clothes.

'I don't know,' Mary Ellen replied. 'But I hope it's not Pearl because she's . . .' She broke off with a frightened look on her face as at that moment a rather tall, elegant girl, Pearl Prescott, with flame red hair and a superior expression swept into the chalet.

'Oh, so you're here, Mary Ellen. West Sussex High School's number one lame duck,' Pearl Prescott said cruelly and she flung her suitcase on to the bed by the window. 'I'll have this bed,' she said without asking the other girls if it suited them and lounged back on the bed and rested her head on her hand.

'She thinks she's the cat's whiskers,' Lucy Jane thought. Jasmine gave Lucy Jane a quick look and

Mary Ellen bent her head trying to hold back the tears.

'Well, I hope we'll all be friends,' Lucy Jane said tentatively, trying to break the icy atmosphere.

'I doubt it,' Pearl said without giving the girls a glance. 'I've no time for friends. I'm here to work. I want to become a star,' she said. Then she added, 'And I did not expect to be put into the same room, chalet, cottage, cabin or whatever this silly hut is called with my school's number one beauty queen and goody-goody.' And with that she did an arabesque and said, 'See. You'll never see a higher or straighter leg than that.' And she pirouetted out of the room.

'Great rolling tiger's eyes,' Jasmine said, her eyebrows raised to the sky. Lucy Jane added, 'Great nothing. She's just a great swank.'

Mary Ellen suddenly whispered, her head bowed, 'I was hoping I wouldn't be in the same room as Pearl. But now I am,' and she started to cry.

'Don't worry,' Lucy Jane said comfortingly. 'We'll help you make the best of it.'

Jasmine put her arm round Mary Ellen. 'Some people don't have any godliness,' she continued shaking her head. 'Some people like to say cruel things. Lucy Jane and I know. She gets teased because of her glasses and I get teased because of my hair.'

The important thing for all the students was that they were to be taught so many new ways of improving their dancing. Things that Lucy Jane had never even thought would be good for her were on the timetable. Each day either before lunch or tea, the girls had an exercise class in the pool to strengthen their muscles.

So once a day in their swimsuits they did the same *barre* exercises as in the class, but in the water, holding on to the side of the pool.

'The resistance of the water against your legs will build up your muscles, so everything will become easier when you are back in the ballet studio,' the ballet mistress, Miss Duval, told them.

Two days a week there were mime classes. Here the girls were taught ballet language. By using their hands instead of their voices they could express themselves and tell a story.

The first movement Lucy Jane learnt meant 'beautiful girl', and to express this she had to use the back of her hand and let it softly encircle her face, being careful not to let her hand touch her face or look stiff. Then the girls learnt how to say 'married' by pointing with arms stretched to the fourth finger on their left hand.

When Miss Duval said, 'Brisk walk for all you girls tomorrow morning at 7.00 before breakfast,' Lucy Jane was amazed. 'A fast walk will increase your stamina, so you won't get so out of breath in class,' Miss Duval finished.

Although Lucy Jane didn't know if this was true or not, she was so anxious to do everything to improve her dancing that she joined in the early morning walks with great enthusiasm.

Despite the arrival of Pearl, Lucy Jane felt sure that the dancing camp was going to be a terrific adventure. If Pearl made trouble Angela would put her in her place, as Angela wasn't frightened of anyone.

7

The Very Important Guest

The camp was set in the grounds of a large old country house. The main building was the big house itself, where the offices and ballet studios were situated. The dining-hall was a sort of Nissen hut, and all the bedrooms were in the little chalets. There was a separate cottage where the nurse and doctor were always at the ready, in case of an accident.

The first few days Lucy Jane, Angela, Jasmine and Mary Ellen all tried very hard to become friends with Pearl. But Pearl kept herself to herself and didn't even try to be nice.

Most days, before breakfast the children did what was called an early morning 'wake up, work out, warm up', that is, if they weren't doing exercises in the pool. The 'wake up' was rather like PE class, and none of the children took it very seriously, although they all found it enjoyable.

Lucy Jane and her friends settled into life on the camp fairly easily and in their spare time wrote letters home, phoned their parents and tried to get used to being away. But usually when there was free time Mary Ellen was nowhere to be found, and when Lucy Jane and Jasmine searched for her they found her all alone in the swimming pool. She was wearing a rubber exercise belt strapped round her waist to support her back, and was doing special exercises for her legs in the water.

'I have to do these exercises for my bad leg,' Mary Ellen puffed, 'otherwise it gets weaker and I can't manage the Scottish dancing.'

'Don't you find it tiring doing all this extra work?' Lucy Jane enquired.

'Oh, I'm used to it,' Mary Ellen answered, philosophically, as she continued to move her leg back and forth. 'Better to do extra exercises than not be able to walk properly, or miss the chance of being in the competition.'

Jasmine and Lucy Jane looked at her full of admiration. 'You're really special,' Lucy Jane said to her warmly, and they left the pool to let Mary Ellen continue her exercises.

When they were outside Lucy Jane commented, 'I suppose it's like the *barre* practice we do in the pool, to improve our strength and muscles, except poor Mary Ellen has to do it every day of her life.'

Lucy Jane woke early one morning and noticed that Pearl had already dressed and left the room. When Lucy Jane started to collect up her ballet clothes she noticed little bits of grit in the bottom of her ballet shoes. 'Oh, bother,' she said as she shook out the tiny stone chips. 'How did those get in there?' But she forgot about it when Jasmine said, 'I've finished in the bathroom. Who's next?'

Mary Ellen went in to clean her teeth. 'Will you wait for me?' she called from behind the door.

''Course we will,' Lucy Jane said kindly. 'We're your friends aren't we?'

Mary Ellen laughed happily and nodded to herself hoping it was true.

Then the three girls set off to the dining-hall for the 'wake up'. Suddenly Jasmine stopped and exclaimed, 'Oh, my toe cap has come off my tap shoe. How on earth did that happen? How am I going to put it back on again? They were my best tap shoes and I have two tap classes this morning.' Jasmine was very, very upset. She knew she couldn't dance without her shoes.

Lucy Jane looked at Jasmine's shoe and thought how strange it was that they both had something happen to their shoes, and she said, 'Better get one of the teachers to give you a hammer or screwdriver or something.'

When they were nearly at the dining-hall they saw Angela waiting outside to greet them. She was already dressed in her Scottish dancing clothes. 'Don't I look like a banana dressed like this?'

'No, you look really good,' Lucy Jane said, looking down at Angela's soft black leather cross-laced shoes and white stockings. 'Won't you spoil your shoes?'

Lucy Jane asked, concerned that Angela's light dancing shoes might get spoiled on the grass.

'Suppose I may,' Angela said. 'But you know me, wicked, wicked, wicked,' and she laughed infectiously. Jasmine, Mary Ellen and Lucy Jane all laughed too. Angela's sweet freckled face smiled cheekily at them and they forgot all about their own shoes.

As it had started to rain all the girls went into the great huge hall for their 'wake and stretch' or 'wake up, work out, warm up'. The music on the loudspeaker kept stopping as it wasn't working properly and by the end of the half-hour work out all the children were falling about laughing helplessly including Jasmine, Mary Ellen, Lucy Jane and, needless to say, most of all Angela.

'That was terrific,' Angela said as they left the dining-hall after breakfast. 'I haven't had such a good laugh since I was born.' And she skipped and turned along the path, happy that it was no longer raining.

'Well, better go and learn how to be a Scottish princess,' she said, winking, and away she ran.

'My class is in the studio in the main house today,' Lucy Jane said.

'So is mine,' Jasmine added. 'Where are you, Mary Ellen?'

'I'm in the same place as Angela today so I'd better run along. At least I have a real friend there,' she said.

'She's a peanut butter and jelly person. You'll never find a truer friend than Angela,' Lucy Jane laughed.

Mary Ellen nodded and laughed too and made her way as best she could to catch up Angela at the Tara hall for national and Scottish dancing.

63

That evening as Lucy Jane, Angela, Jasmine and Mary Ellen walked back from the dining-hall Lucy Jane suddenly said, 'Do you think the boys from the tennis camp next door are doing these things to our shoes to annoy us?'

'Why should they? They're only here for tennis and anyway they'd have to climb in. We've never seen them,' Angela replied logically.

After breakfast the following morning Lucy Jane took Angela to one side. 'Some strange things happened again last night, noises, things missing, ballet shoes and things,' Lucy Jane said nervously.

'Oh, orange pips, you're turning into a baby. But if you're really worried, why don't we take it in turns to keep watch on your chalet and see if anyone goes there?'

'But we'd have to make an excuse not to do our dancing class,' Lucy Jane replied, not liking the idea of missing a ballet lesson.

'Of course,' Angela said. 'We've got to do a 24-hour watch so between us we'll see everyone who goes into the room, and I don't care missing a dancing class one bit!' And she laughed.

That afternoon, Angela went to her teacher and said, 'Sorry, Miss McNeil, can't do Scottish dancing this afternoon. Hurt me knee.'

Miss McNeil looked down at Angela's leg and was surprised to see a large bandage around Angela's knee. Angela lifted up her leg and said, 'Bashed me knee on me way to the dining-hall.'

'Oh dear,' Miss McNeil sympathised. 'It does look bad. Well, if you can't dance then you'd better watch.

And by the way, Angela dear,' she added kindly. 'I keep reminding you it's *my knee* and not *me knee*. Try to remember. It sounds so much better. We Scottish lassies must stick together.' She smiled at Angela and again looked at her knee.

'Oh no, Miss McNeil. Can't watch,' Angela answered immediately. 'The nurse said I should go to my room and rest,' she continued, making up every word.

'Well,' Miss McNeil replied rather reluctantly, 'if that's what she thinks is best then you'd better go.' And Angela hopped away as quickly as she could before the teacher had time to change her mind.

Once she was out of sight she ran like the wind to her room to take up her position to peep through the curtain and keep watch. She waited patiently for at least an hour, then suddenly Angela saw Pearl dart into the chalet with what looked like a couple of candles and a little tin box in her hand. Angela kept her eyes glued to the window, but to her annoyance she couldn't see a thing once Pearl had shut the door.

'Oh, knicker legs,' Angela said crossly. 'Can't see. Best go and have a look.'

So she tiptoed along to Lucy Jane's chalet where she heard a tapping sound. She was just about to look through the window when she heard Pearl say, 'That'll fix it.' Then Pearl opened the door, and before Angela could hide, Pearl had run away carrying a pair of ballet shoes without even noticing Angela standing a few metres away.

'I suppose she just came to collect her shoes,' Angela thought. 'I'd better wait to see who else comes along.'

But no one did and Angela was rather disappointed that she wasn't about to solve the mystery that afternoon.

Suddenly Lucy Jane came rushing up. 'Guess what?' she asked breathlessly. 'Pearl came into the ballet class with a pair of ballet shoes and *hid them inside the piano*. Then she said she had forgotten her ballet shoes and had to go and collect another pair. Eventually she came back with *a new* pair of shoes.'

Angela listened amazed. 'That's it,' she screamed. 'That's it,' she cried excitedly.

'What?' Lucy Jane asked bewildered.

Angela took Lucy Jane's arm and dragged her inside her room. She was almost too excited to talk. 'Pearl came here this afternoon,' she started in a hoarse whisper, 'and she had what looked like some candles and a tin. Then she left with some ballet shoes saying, "That'll fix it".'

The two girls looked at each other. Lucy Jane opened her eyes wide. 'We'll have to wait and see if anything else goes wrong,' Lucy Jane said excitedly. 'I think it's brilliant.'

'Won't be so brilliant if she's put candle grease on your toothbrush,' Angela said in her down-to-earth way.

'Suppose not,' Lucy Jane agreed.

For the time being all the detective work was forgotten. After supper a famous Russian ballet dancer and ballet mistress were coming to the camp to give a talk and demonstration in the main house.

Although Angela and Mary Ellen weren't really interested in ballet, Lucy Jane and Jasmine persuaded them to come along to the demonstration with them. So when they had eaten all the girls crowded into the big ballet studio in the main house. They huddled together sitting on wooden chairs or on the floor or

leaning against the *barre* to watch Tamara
Trochkanova give the demonstration and Madame
Sèdowa teach. Many of the girls scraped back their
hair into pony tails or buns so that they looked like
ballerinas, and sat very straight or stood with their feet
turned out. When Madame Sèdowa, who must have
been at least eighty, turned their way they stood or sat
even straighter.

They were all a little nervous for fear that they might
be asked to stand up and dance. Lucy Jane's heart was
beating really fast until Madame Sèdowa said, 'I vod
like von of ze girls to dance, but sorry no much room.'

After that Lucy Jane relaxed relieved that she
wouldn't have to dance and enjoyed watching the
grace, precision and long stretch of Tamara
Trochkanova. The ballerina was dressed in pink tights,
woolly leg warmers and a torn pink cardigan which she
wore crossed over her black leotard and tied at the back
as she danced part of the Black Swan solo in *Swan
Lake*.

Every so often Madame Sèdowa would hurry across
the room and stop the ballerina by tapping her with a
little thin cane. Then she would explain to the girls
how important it was to interpret the Black Swan with
arrogance and inner wickedness.

'Bad Black Swan in *Swan Lake* pretend to be good
White Swan that prince love. The audience must see ze
happy look on Black Swan's face as she makes ze
prince fall in love with her and not ze White Swan.'

Once the demonstration was over Lucy Jane rushed
up to the ballerina, her cheeks pink and her eyes glazed
over with admiration. She stood by the great star, and

the other girls followed and also crowded round
Tamara Tochkanova. The ballerina smiled down at
them and then patted one or two of the girls on the
head including Lucy Jane. Lucy Jane was thrilled and
managed to say in a small voice, 'It was beautiful, the
best dancing I have ever seen.'

Miss Tamara said, 'Thank you,' and suddenly
handed Lucy Jane her ballet shoes. 'A little souvenir of
Russian dancing,' she said, and again the ballerina
smiled. Then she wrapped her pink woolly shawl

around her shoulders and waved goodbye and was gone. Lucy Jane held the shoes to her chest amazed, tears of joy in her eyes. Then she skipped off excitedly to the chalet with all the girls.

They forgot all about the mystery of the ballet and tap shoes, their hearts were so full of the thrill and excitement of seeing the great Russian ballerina and teacher. Lucy Jane clasped the shoes with a dreamy look in her eyes and said, 'Her *arabesque* was so high, her arms were so graceful when she jumped, she went into the air like a bird and landed like a feather. I want to be like that some day. I want to dance on point and do thirty-two *fouettés* on the same spot like Tamara Trochkanova.'

Jasmine laughed affectionately. 'Oh, you are a dreamer,' she said. But Lucy Jane didn't hear. She laid her head on the pillow, Tamara Trochkanova's ballet shoes still in her hands. 'Yes,' she thought, 'a ballerina, that's what I want to be. I want to work so hard and dance so well that I can perform at Covent Garden and in Moscow and New York – I want to be like Tamara Trochkanova.'

8

Telling the Truth

The following day Pearl left the room long before the others had even finished getting dressed. Jasmine, Mary Ellen and Lucy Jane were still putting on their jeans and collecting their clothes.

'I've got to try really hard today,' Mary Ellen said, putting her shoes and white socks into the little cloth bag with her initials on. 'We're doing a final week exam and if I don't do well, I doubt if I'll be allowed to be in the Golden Star Festival.'

'We've got a sort of exam as well,' Lucy Jane said as she finished sewing the pink satin ribbons on her new pink satin ballet shoes, and put them into her lunch box.

'Let's hope we all do well,' Jasmine joined in, as she too had a test that day.

As Lucy Jane arrived at her ballet class she was rather pleased to have a test as she felt she had really made a lot of progress since she arrived at the camp.

She hoped when she got home Miss Sweetfoot would think she had improved too, especially her *entrechats* and her *arabesques*. But when she slipped on her new ballet shoes, she was annoyed that they weren't comfortable and wondered what was wrong. She thought maybe she had left the needle inside the shoes and she checked to see, but she hadn't. When she reached the *barre* she suddenly started to limp, her foot hurt so much. But she ignored the horrid feeling, thinking it was because the shoes were new, and began the class with everyone else.

Suddenly she stopped in her tracks. There on the other side of the room was Tamara Trochkanova sitting with her head tilted to one side, dressed in a dark blue and white dress. Had Miss Tamara come to see them dance? Was she really going to watch the class? Lucy Jane could hardly swallow she was so surprised. To Lucy Jane's annoyance the pain in her foot got worse and she found it impossible to work properly.

Finally it was so bad that she had to say to the teacher, 'Excuse me, Miss Duval. My feet, my shoes or something are hurting me terribly,' and she limped to the side of the studio and took off her shoes, examined the inside and rubbed her feet.

'Oh no!' she exclaimed, as she noticed a little tiny nail lodged in the sole of her ballet shoe. 'How on earth did that get there?' She tried to pull the nail out, but it was firmly embedded in the sole of her shoe. 'The point of the nail has been digging up into my foot,' she whispered to herself. It was a wonder that it hadn't gone right through into Lucy Jane's flesh. If it had, Lucy Jane certainly wouldn't have been able to dance again for some time.

'Why did such an embarrassing thing have to happen in front of Miss Tamara?' she wondered.

'What on earth's going on?' Miss Duval said impatiently to Lucy Jane, who was struggling to get the small nail out of the sole of her shoe. 'This is no way to impress me or Tamara Trochkanova. I've asked Miss Trochkanova here especially to see my most promising girls.'

'I'm very sorry,' Lucy Jane said meekly, 'but somehow there's a nail in the bottom of my shoe and I don't know how it got there.'

Miss Duval took Lucy Jane's shoe to examine it. She pulled out the tiny copper nail. 'Oh,' she said, surprised when the nail was in her hand. 'This is one of the nails I had in a little tin on the piano last week to use to tack down the piano felt. How it got here I can't imagine,' and she looked at the minute nail, mystified.

When Lucy Jane heard the word 'tin', suddenly everything started to click into place. Angela had seen Pearl with a tin *and* she had heard a tapping noise. *Pearl* had to be the person who was playing all those horrid tricks on them to try and stop Jasmine, Mary Ellen and Lucy Jane entering the Golden Star Dancing Festival.

But Lucy Jane knew better than to let Pearl know she knew her secret. She danced as if nothing had happened, in fact better than ever before.

At the end of the class Miss Tamara pointed to Lucy Jane and two other girls and said, 'These girls are most delightful, pleasing young dancers. When a little older they should come to Russia, make exchange with Russian girls for study more serious ballet.' She looked at the girls and said, 'Yes? Yes?' she said again. Lucy Jane's eyes grew wide with surprise and excitement.

Then Miss Tamara chucked Lucy Jane under the chin and said, 'I hope to see more of you. Work hard and I know I will see the "big ballerina Lucy Jane" one day. Remember, I expect to see you dance in Russia before I am old.'

These words made Lucy Jane feel dizzy with happiness. She forgot all about the bad start to the class and the nail in her shoe. Now all she could think of was being called 'big ballerina Lucy Jane' one day.

Meanwhile, Mary Ellen was having her own adventures on the other side of the camp. No sooner had Mary Ellen started to dance her first reel of the day than she slipped and had to be helped to the side of the room.

Her teacher was most upset. 'Mary Ellen,' Miss McNeil said, 'my prize Scottish dancer, what's the matter?'

'I don't know,' Mary Ellen replied fighting back the tears. 'My shoes are so slippery I can hardly stand up.' It was especially hard for Mary Ellen as she could only use the ball of her right foot and her balance needed to be particulary good as she couldn't use her heel. Her teacher looked at her shoes amazed, and said, 'Why did you rub this grease on the bottom of your shoes, dear?'

Angela, who was watching all this, immediately rushed over to Miss McNeil and said, 'I think I know how the grease got there. I think it is candle wax. Please can I talk to you at the end of the class?'

Miss McNeil nodded and said to Mary Ellen, 'Better wash or scrape it off before you dance again, Mary Ellen dear. Now run along. We'll wait for you.' And Mary Ellen limped to the cloakroom as fast as she could to wash the bottom of her black leather Scottish dancing shoes.

When the class was over Angela stayed behind to talk to Miss McNeil. She asked if Mary Ellen could stay behind to talk, too.

'Now, what is all this, girls?' Miss McNeil asked, concerned.

Mary Ellen and Angela looked at each other. Mary Ellen wasn't at all sure that Angela should say what was the matter, but Angela turned to Mary Ellen and said, 'Listen, me old twinkle toes, it's better to tell the truth, because somebody could get badly hurt if we don't.'

At that moment Lucy Jane came rushing into the room looking for them. 'Guess what, guess what?' she said breathlessly, not noticing Miss McNeil. Lucy Jane suddenly stopped when she saw Miss McNeil. 'Oh, I'm sorry,' she said politely. 'I didn't know you were still working.'

'We're not,' Angela said firmly. 'We're telling the truth.'

'Now, come on, you three,' Miss McNeil said patiently. 'Let's get all this mystery out in the open,' and Angela began to tell the whole story.

Miss McNeil didn't want to believe that Pearl had done this any more than the girls wanted to tell her, but she felt the whole case was serious and said, 'I shall have to take this to higher authority. Spitefulness, teasing, bullying or cruelty of any kind is abhorrent. This is not what I would expect from any girl who is interested in an artistic life. I am very upset if Pearl Prescott really is at the bottom of this.'

Mary Ellen was upset too, as she was at school with Pearl and she didn't want to make life even more difficult for herself when she got back to school next term.

Lucy Jane, Angela and Mary Ellen all looked at each other and then back at Miss McNeil, wondering what she was going to say or do next.

'You won't do anything to Pearl, will you?' Lucy Jane asked, worried that their chalet mate might get into trouble.

'I hope she does,' Angela said sensibly. 'She's been horrid to all three of you, and you're my friends and anyone who's horrid to you deserves to get into trouble.'

Miss McNeil interrupted: 'Run along, girls. Say no more about this to anyone and leave it all to me to sort out.'

So the three girls walked off in search of Jasmine to tell her the news.

Jasmine was waiting for them by the dining-hall entrance, holding her tap shoes and looking very upset. 'Where've you been?' she asked almost in tears. 'I've been looking for you as Pearl has really upset me saying they won't let black girls into the competition.'

Lucy Jane immediately put her arm round Jasmine and hugged her. She could see that Jasmine was about to cry.

Then Angela piped in, 'Why did you take any notice of her? She's a wicked old bat, and you should know better than to believe her nonsense. Everyone knows that *anyone* can enter the competition. They can't stop you because of the colour of your skin.' Then she suddenly added, 'They can't stop *me* 'cos I've got red hair, come from Scotland and speak funny.'

'That's true,' Lucy Jane agreed. 'All they are interested in is how well you can dance, and since you tap wonderfully you may win.'

At this, Jasmine cheered up and smiled and when they were all sure Jasmine was really feeling better, Angela said in a hushed voice, 'Now we'd better tell you our news. We think we know who the troublemaker is.'

Jasmine opened her eyes wide as Lucy Jane whispered the name in her ear. Then Mary Ellen said solemnly, 'There's worse to come.' As soon as Mary Ellen had finished Lucy Jane jumped up and down to get everyone's attention. 'Listen,' she said, 'I've got some really special news.' The three girls looked at her and waited.

'Something much more exciting than these silly tricks has happened,' Lucy Jane continued. 'Something really wonderful.'

The girls waited.

'Miss Tamara Tochkanova came to our test today, and she watched us dance,' Lucy Jane went on ecstatically, 'and she was really pleased with me.' Lucy

Jane was too modest to repeat all the compliments. But she looked so happy they all forgot about their problems and hurried off arm in arm to change for supper.

The next morning Lucy Jane woke very early. She lay in bed thinking about her mother and father and brother and how nice it was that she would see them in a few days. It was strange that she hadn't missed them as much as she thought she would. She decided it was mainly because of Jasmine, Angela and Mary Ellen, and also a dream that Tamara Trochkanova had made seem possible.

As Lucy Jane lay awake thinking, she suddenly thought about Pearl. She was very good at ballet, so why did she have to spoil the others' chances in order to do better herself? What joy could she get from being so unkind? And how would she have felt if Mary Ellen had broken her leg, or Lucy Jane had had a septic or poisoned foot, or Jasmine had left the camp because she was so upset? All these questions were going round and round in Lucy Jane's head when Pearl suddenly leapt out of bed. Lucy Jane lay silently, waiting to see what she would do. Lucy Jane was amazed when Pearl started to pack her suitcase. Then she got dressed, flung open the door, put all her bags outside and woke up all three girls to announce, 'I'm going. I have no intention of sharing a room with the three stupidest girls in the camp. I've rung my parents and I'm leaving today.' She slammed the door of the chalet and disappeared.

Lucy Jane, Jasmine and Mary Ellen immediately sat

up in bed and looked at each other, amazed. In their hearts they were relieved and pleased that Pearl had decided to go. Was she afraid of being discovered?

Lucy Jane scrambled out of bed and whispered excitedly, 'I'm going to tell Angela.' She ran out of the chalet and tapped on the next door chalet. 'Angela. Quick, quick,' Lucy Jane said, still in her nightie. 'Pearl has packed her cases and gone.'

'Oh!' Angela said laughing. 'I thought if you were going to wake me it would at least be to tell me Tamara Trochkanova had given you her *tutu*. Anyway,' she continued, 'if Pearl's gone it's good riddance to bad rubbish.'

'But why?' Lucy Jane asked, worried.

'Because the silly moo knows she's been found out.'

'Well, let's hope that's the last we see or hear of Pearl,' said Angela.

9

The Gift

Once Jasmine and Lucy Jane were ready they rushed off to the pool to do their water exercises. When they were in the pool and the music had begun and they were working hard, holding on to the side of the pool, chest deep in water doing their *battements tendues*, Angela suddenly appeared at the side of the pool. She was dressed in a *tutu*, with a rose between her teeth held high on the shoulders of two boys from the boys'

tennis camp next door. They were dressed in striped, old-fashioned long bathing suits, and had painted moustaches, and were holding Angela in a silly position pretending they were ballet dancers.

All the girls in the pool started to giggle, as Angela was waltzed round the pool, a solemn expression on her face. Her arms were at a strange angle and looked wonderfully ridiculous as she pretended to be a ballerina.

Eventually the girls could ignore the sight of Angela and the boys no longer, and there was hysterical laughter, especially when the teacher tried to shoo all three away, and chased them round and round the side of the pool. But the boys were too quick. Suddenly with a great '*Olé!*' they threw Angela into the pool. Then the two boys divebombed into the pool after her, making an enormous splash. All the girls screamed, as they were drenched and their hair got wet. At that point, everyone was jumping about and splashing and playing the fool. But Miss Johns was getting more and more cross. She tried to regain control of the class. But Angela and the two boys couldn't hear what she was saying and were still doing handstands and clowning around. Suddenly, Miss Johns slipped and fell into the pool herself. For a moment there was an enormous burst of laughter, and then hush as Miss Johns emerged dripping wet and looking even crosser.

'Now Angela's for it,' Lucy Jane whispered to Jasmine through her giggles. She clasped on to Jasmine's arm fearful of what might happen to Angela. But to everyone's amazement Miss Johns started to laugh too, and turned round to the girls and said, 'I think we can safely say that this class is well and truly over for today, and all I can suggest is that we give those *three naughty clowns* a round of applause and tell them not to disrupt our pool exercise class again.'

Everyone cheered and clapped as Angela and the boys made their way out of the pool, bowing and waving as they went, to get ready for breakfast.

After breakfast the four friends were asked to go and see the principal of the camp in her office in the main house. Was it about Pearl? When they reached the office door Mary Ellen said, 'I wish I didn't have to be here, as I go to the same school as Pearl and she could make things so hard for me next term if I say anything now.'

'Don't you worry,' Angela said firmly. 'I'll do all the talking,' and she took Mary Ellen's hand to make sure she went into the office with her. Jasmine and Lucy Jane followed reluctantly. When they got into the office Miss Margaret, the principal of the summer camp, smartly dressed in a blue flowered frock, stood up and said, 'Come in, girls. Please sit down. I believe we have a little talking to do.'

The four girls tentatively made their way into the office, sat down and waited for Miss Margaret to speak again. There was a silence as the girls looked round the sparsely furnished room until suddenly Angela stood up and said, 'There's been a lot of trouble, and these are my friends and they don't want to say anything, but I think you should know the truth.'

Miss Margaret settled down to listen. 'Very well, Angela,' she said. 'You tell me all that's been going on. Before you begin, let me say we've made our own enquiries from her dancing teacher, and we now know a lot more about Pearl Prescott than we did two weeks ago.'

When Angela had finished explaining all the dramas Miss Margaret said, 'Well, girls, I'm really sorry you have been through all this and I hope your stay here has not been spoiled. But as it happened, Pearl's parents rang us last night and said Pearl wanted to leave this morning.' She looked at the girls and waited for their reaction, then continued, 'It means we won't have to take any action that would affect you. Mary Ellen, you won't have to worry when you go back to school. You can all feel happy that the reason she has gone has nothing to do with you.' Miss Margaret looked rather pleased that it all had been settled so easily.

'But she still tried to ruin our stay,' Lucy Jane said boldly.

'Yes,' Mary Ellen and Jasmine agreed. 'We didn't want her to go, just to stop her being horrid.'

'Well, she's gone now,' Miss Margaret said flicking her pencil. 'And her parents know what has happened here. Whether they wish to believe it or not is another matter. However,' she said standing up and changing the subject, 'on a brighter note, you have all individually done extremely well. All four of you have shown great promise, have worked really hard and I'm sure those of you who have entered the Golden Star Festival will have great success.' And she showed the girls to the door, but asked Lucy Jane to stay behind.

Then she gently took Lucy Jane's arm and pulled her to one side. 'I thought I should mention that we have been watching you.' Lucy Jane looked up concerned. Then Miss Margaret continued, 'We have been very pleased with your progress. As you know,

Miss Trochkanova was most impressed by your dancing and feels you should seriously consider taking it up professionally. That is, if you don't grow too tall.'

Although Lucy Jane didn't like the last remark, she looked up and smiled. 'Thank you, Miss Margaret,' she said. Just as she was leaving the room she added, 'Miss Tamara gave me her shoes,' and she slipped from the room, a new and special feeling filling her heart.

On the last night all the girls and the boys from the tennis camp were invited to a camp-fire party barbecue and sing-song.

There was going to be a double treat for the girls because they had already planned a midnight feast in Lucy Jane's chalet and they had been saving up biscuits and fruit from the dining-hall for the past few days.

At six o'clock the girls and boys were divided into groups to build the fires, light the barbecue and cook the food. By eight-thirty the fires were roaring, the food was cooking and most of the girls were huddled together chatting about ballet, jazz and modern dancing and the boys were sauntering around serving a fruit punch.

By nine-thirty it was nearly dark and the fires were still blazing and the boys and girls were sitting together singing songs round the fire.

It was a clear sky and the stars and moon looked so beautiful and bright, suddenly one of the boys took off all his clothes except his underpants and started doing an American Indian war dance. He was joined by

89

another boy. Their silhouettes against the flames were a marvellous sight, but the teachers in charge shouted for everyone to pack up, put the fires out and go to bed. The boys left for the next-door camp with as much noise as they could manage. So as the fires were beaten down to a cinder, water was thrown on the embers and the last wisps of smoke rose from the ground, the girls crept away for their midnight feast.

Angela had to wait until after the teacher's room

check, before she crept over to Lucy Jane's chalet.

As they sat on the floor and shared out the food by torchlight, they felt sure that they heard someone at the door. Angela quickly turned off the torch. They sat for a moment in the dark not daring to move.

Jasmine jumped up to check the curtains were closed properly and listened to hear if there was anyone outside. When she thought it was all clear she crept back and switched on again.

Mary Ellen said, 'You've all been so kind to me, I'd like to give you something to remind us all of this stay at the camp.' And she took her pearl necklace from her suitcase. 'This is rather long for me, so let's break it, divide the pearls into four so we can each make a pearl bracelet to remind us of the holiday and turn Pearl into a good memory.'

The three girls looked at each other, very touched, then Angela said, 'Mary Ellen, we don't want a pearl necklace. We're just happy that we're all friends.'

'No,' Mary Ellen insisted. 'I want to think that one day we may all be wearing these bracelets when we're doing different things in different parts of the world and then we can remember this summer camp.'

It was such a lovely thought that Lucy Jane gave Mary Ellen a hug, and said, 'We are so lucky to have met you. You're so nice and you never grumble or complain.'

'That's why I like you so much,' Mary Ellen said quietly, 'because you don't mention my leg and you treat me the same as everyone else.'

'But you are the same,' Lucy Jane said firmly. 'Even better. Angela says you're the best girl in the Scottish

91

dancing class and that your sword dance is *brilliant*.'

Mary Ellen said, 'Thank you.' Then she carefully divided the beads into four piles. They packed up the remains of the feast and prepared to go to bed, each girl feeling very happy. They all knew when they were going to wear the bracelets.

10

The Setback

When it was time for the girls to pack their bags, although they were looking forward to going home and seeing their parents again, they were sad at the thought of parting from each other.

'Now,' Lucy Jane said as she, Mary Ellen, Jasmine and Angela stood by their suitcases waiting for the coach to pick them up to go to the station, 'we've got to continue to work really hard so we're all definitely in the Golden Star Festival.' Then she added happily, 'Wearing our pearl bracelets.' All the girls agreed and hugged each other.

When Lucy Jane arrived home that evening it was like returning to paradise. 'I loved being at the camp. We met Tamara Trochkanova, the Russian ballerina. She gave me her ballet shoes and told Miss Margaret I show promise,' Lucy Jane said to her mother when she had finished her supper, 'and she told me I should go to Russia and . . .' Lucy Jane didn't finish. 'But I'm really happy to be home.' She jumped down from her chair and gave her mother a squeeze. Her mother kissed her hair and looked down into her daughter's smiling face. It seemed as if she had grown up so much in the short time she had been away.

'I'm happy to have you home,' her mother said gently. 'We all missed you.'

'A lot,' Jeremy added from behind his mug of milk. 'Tremely a lot.'

'Where did you learn such big words?' Lucy Jane said, laughing.

'Mummy,' Jeremy answered shyly.

Lucy Jane immediately gave him a kiss and lifted him off his chair, happy that the rest of the holidays would be spent with her family.

When Lucy Jane returned to school, life once again took on the demanding routine of schoolwork, homework, ballet lessons and extra dancing classes. But in no time at all the buzz and excitement of preparing for the dancing festival began. They were doing extra dancing practice after school each day, their parents were making the costumes. Lucy Jane needed only one costume for the competition and that was a ballet dress. Jasmine too needed only one costume – a red, black and white sequinned top hat and tails outfit. But for the first part of the competition all the competitors had to wear leotards and tights.

'I can hardly sleep at nights,' Jasmine confessed to Lucy Jane at school one morning. 'Making my costume is so exciting and it's so beautiful, I dream about it all night.'

'It is exciting,' Lucy Jane agreed. She too had been lying awake and thinking about her beautiful blue and

white ballet dress and wondering what it would be like actually to be taking part in the competition. How much did she really want to win?

One day, as the day of the competition drew nearer, Lucy Jane said to Jasmine as they were going in to school lunch, 'Do you know what my dream would be?'

'No,' said Jasmine.

'My dream,' Lucy Jane said slowly, 'would be that you and Mary Ellen would be the winners of your

95

section. Angela and I would get a prize for *trying*. Still, someone horrid may win,' said Lucy Jane gloomily. 'Because sometimes that's life. Life isn't fair. Unfair and horrid things happen to people all the time. People have to learn to accept and live with the horrid things.'

'You sound like my mother,' Jasmine said. 'When I say things aren't fair, she says, "Black or white, darling, you're going to have to learn to live in a world that is unfair," and I suppose it's true.'

The following morning at breakfast Mrs Tadworth looked very worried.

'Oh, Lucy darling, I don't know how to tell you this, but I think Jeremy's got mumps. If he has, it means you will be in quarantine and won't be able to be in the festival.'

Lucy Jane looked up at her mother aghast. Her mouth fell open and she couldn't speak.

Not to dance in the festival was the worst and most awful thing that could happen to her. For a moment she felt angry with her brother for getting the mumps and furious with herself for feeling so upset.

She lowered her head and fiddled with the toast on her plate feeling that her whole world had fallen apart. She was in such a black mood after breakfast that she didn't even bother to go up to her room to do her *barre* exercises.

This was the first term that Lucy Jane had gone to school on her own, and when her mother heard the front door slam she knew Lucy Jane had set off for the bus stop without waiting for her father or saying good-bye. So Mrs Tadworth rushed to the door and

called after her, 'I'll collect you from school as usual.'
Then she watched her daughter's sad figure stomp
gloomily down the road to the bus stop.

As the preparations for the festival continued, Lucy
Jane only participated half-heartedly, still waiting to
know if her brother's swollen cheeks would develop
into mumps. She did feel sorry for him as he had to
stay in bed and no one, including the doctor, seemed to
know if he had swollen glands or mumps.

That evening after school Lucy Jane decided to
telephone her grandmother and pour out her heart.

'Don't tell me you're not practising, dearie, just
because you may be in quarantine for mumps.' She
paused for a long time and Lucy Jane thought they had
been cut off.

'Are you there, Granny?' Lucy Jane asked in a
worried tone.

'Yes, dearie, I'm thinking.' Then she suddenly said,

'I think both you and your mummy are very silly.'

'What do you mean?' Lucy Jane asked surprised.

'Well, dearie,' Lucy Jane's granny said at last, 'you *had* mumps when you were staying with me when you were little, and you and Mummy and Daddy came to stay before Jeremy was born. Don't you remember?' Lucy Jane had forgotten.

'Your mother and father went to the Edinburgh Festival for six days and while they were away you had the mumps, and when they came home they could hardly believe it, as you didn't have any swelling left at all.'

'Is this true, Granny?'

'Yes, dear.'

''Bye, Granny, must telephone the girls to tell them I'm not in quarantine even if Jeremy does get mumps,' and she blew a kiss down the phone and then started to dial Angela.

Angela, who was not always one to give as much time as she should to practice, was in the kitchen at the back of her parents' newsagent's shop when the telephone rang. She was on the kitchen table demonstrating to her mother how neatly she could dance the sword dance.

'It's for you, Angela,' her mother said as she tried to hand the telephone to her daughter, who was still dancing on the table in her soft black Scottish dancing shoes. Angela took the phone.

'Oh, hello, orange pips, what's your trouble?' Angela asked Lucy Jane as she sat on the table's edge and swung her legs back and forth while Lucy Jane told her her news.

'Good,' Angela said. 'Got to go now. I'm practising, believe it or not. I'm showing me mum how neat and light I can do me sword dance.'

When Lucy Jane rang Mary Ellen the housekeeper said Mary Ellen was with the physiotherapist. She was giving her extra exercises to strengthen her leg for the competition.

'Tell her I'm not going to get mumps and I'll see her at the competition,' Lucy Jane said happily. 'Oh yes, and tell her that I'll be wearing the bracelet!'

The housekeeper knew that Lucy Jane was a good friend to Mary Ellen, but she knew too, that it was more than she dare do to disrupt the exercise session. Mary Ellen was building up her strength for the competition.

When Lucy Jane rang Jasmine, Jasmine said, 'Fantastic! You'd better let Miss Sweetfoot know as she's been very worried about you.'

The day of the competition arrived at last and Lucy Jane's three-quarter length white net and white satin ballet dress was only just ready in time. Her mother had been up all evening to finish it. The bodice was a plain white satin, with a lovely neat waistband of pale blue, the sleeves were puffed and made of net and the skirt was all net with blue ribbons looped around the hem. Mrs Tadworth had found sewing the looped ribbons very difficult.

Lucy Jane woke early and rushed around the house collecting her ballet shoes, hair ribbons, hair nets, hair clips, elastic bands, tights, leotard and blue flowers to wear with the ballet dress. She slipped into her

brother's room to see how he was feeling as the doctor
had finally said yes, Jeremy had a mild dose of the
mumps.

'What am I going to put all my clothes into?' Lucy
Jane asked in a panic as she left her brother's room.

'I thought we discussed that yesterday,' her mother said calmly as she followed Lucy Jane along the hall. 'We said we'd put everything into one big case with your name marked on the top. That way it won't get muddled with all the costumes of the other children.'

'All right,' Lucy Jane replied absent-mindedly. 'What about my food?' Lucy Jane asked.

'I've packed it, sweetheart,' her mother said. 'It's all in your lunch box.' Lucy Jane rushed to the kitchen to check the food was in the lunch box.

'Where's the orange juice? If you haven't had time to squeeze it, shall I?' Lucy Jane asked, still fussing about in the kitchen, dithering from one side to the other not really knowing what to do next.

Mrs Tadworth remained calm. 'Let's be sensible, Lucy darling. You've worked very hard and today you're going to show the judges *how* hard you've worked because you're going to be the best you can be.'

'But supposing I forget?' Lucy Jane asked, worried. 'And what about the days I didn't practise so hard, as I thought I'd be in quarantine.'

'You won't forget, because you have learnt the steps of the dance very thoroughly. So please put "forgetting" out of your mind, and start thinking *how good* you're going to be,' Mrs Tadworth said, standing by the kitchen stove. Then she gave her daughter a kiss and an extra hug and said, 'If you want you can take my tiny gold chain with you and wear it round your neck, to remind you you *are* going to be *good*, and as Miss Trochkanova gave you her shoes, I would have thought they too would be a reminder.'

101

Lucy Jane watched her mother take her thin chain from her neck and give it to her. Lucy Jane took the gold chain in her hand and looked at it a moment smiling, happy that her mother had so much confidence in her. 'I'll wear it,' she said and gave her mother a kiss. Some special part of her mother would be with her all day and that, she knew, would be the best lucky charm she could have. And she had the pearl bracelet and the ballet shoes as well.

11

The Competition

When Lucy Jane arrived at the Albert Hall, she saw coach-loads of girls from all over England. Outside the Albert Hall there was a huge red and white banner saying: Golden Star Dancing Festival. The sight of the banner gave Lucy Jane a little buzz of excitement in her tummy. 'This is it,' she thought. Her mother drove round to the back entrance where the children had been told to meet to register their names and be given their numbers and instructions for the competition.

As Lucy Jane struggled out of the car with her big case and lunch box, she suddenly felt very hot. Hot with excitement. Her mother jumped out to help her and said, as she gave Lucy Jane a big hug, 'I'll come and watch the second half this afternoon, after you've done your first compulsory dance.'

'Good,' Lucy Jane replied, happy at the thought that her mother would be there. She gave her mother a wave and struggled with her big case and lunch box to the side door where three officials in green blazers were waiting to greet the girls.

'Name?' one of the men said quickly.

'Lucy Jane,' Lucy Jane answered, her heart beating very fast.

'No surname?' the man replied impatiently.

'Sorry,' Lucy Jane said, feeling sick. 'Tadworth.'

He looked down the list in front of him and eventually said, 'Ah, yes. Tadworth. Number 14.' He gave Lucy Jane two large white pieces of cotton material with a black number 14 printed on each of them, and also four safety pins pinned to one corner.

'Pin these on your costumes and wear them at all times,' he said and waved his hand for Lucy Jane to move on.

'But where do I go?' Lucy Jane asked, worried that she would never find her way in the maze of corridors, rooms and doors going round and round under the stage of the huge round building.

'Look at the list on the blackboard. See which dressing-room number you are and then follow the arrows to your room.'

Lucy Jane fumbled to get out her glasses and looked down the list to see her name. 'I hope I'm in the same dressing-room as Jasmine,' she thought, a little afraid now she was really at the dancing festival in this huge building with no one she knew around to show her the way, not even Miss Sweetfoot. She had imagined it was all going to be exciting and thrilling, but instead it was frightening and lonely because she was one of the first girls to arrive. She looked down at the case at her feet and immediately thought, 'Must get to the dressing-room quickly and hang up my dress, otherwise it'll be all creased.'

Suddenly a large group of girls arrived with their hair in rollers and curlers, each one holding their dresses on hangers covered in plastic bags draped over their shoulders. Lucy Jane looked anxiously to see if there was anyone she knew, but none of the girls from her school had arrived yet, so she followed the arrows to her dressing-room. She knocked timidly on the dressing-room door, then put her head round. But the rather shabby room with faded green paint and broken chairs was empty. Lucy Jane put her glasses on to check the names on the door. Then she suddenly let out a little yelp of happiness, as marked in front of her it said: 'Dressing-room B. *All tap and ballet Grade IV girls*'. That's us, Jasmine, and me, she thought. Then she looked at the label on the adjoining dressing-room door which said: 'All Junior Scottish girls'. Hurray, Lucy Jane thought, all of us friends are close together, and she peeped inside to see if she could see Mary Ellen or Angela. But their dressing-room, which was also huge and faded with old chairs and dusty mirrors, was also empty. Can't be the dressing-room of the stars, Lucy Jane thought as she looked at the shabby room. She was right, as marked on the wall beside her was: *All chorus dressing-rooms only in this area*.

She went back into her room again and unpacked her case. She made a neat little space for herself in front of one of the mirrors, and put out her brush and comb, hair ribbons, clips and flowers, and the blusher for her cheeks that her mother had lent her.

When she looked in the mirror and noticed her mother's tiny gold chain around her neck, she smiled. 'I'm going to be good,' she said to herself looking at the chain. 'And I'm going to remember everything and I'm going to enjoy being here.'

At that moment there was a huge bang at the door and a loud voice screaming, 'Hello, orange pips.' It was Angela.

'I'm so glad to see you, Ange,' she said hugging her enthusiastically. 'I thought I'd never see anyone I knew. Even Miss Sweetfoot hasn't arrived. When did you get here?'

'We just came on the coach.'

'Not all the way from Scotland?' Lucy Jane asked.

'Yes,' Angela said, 'but we arrived last night and stayed in some school until this morning.'

'Why didn't you ring me?' Lucy Jane said. 'You could have stayed with us!'

'Because I didn't know what was happening until it was too late,' Angela said, hanging her costume on the door. 'This is a lark,' she said happily. 'Standing in this famous place where all the royalty have been and famous conductors and orchestras and all.'

'Mmmm,' Lucy Jane agreed.

Suddenly more children arrived and wherever you looked there were hoardes of girls in curlers holding ballet dresses and flowered skirts or sequinned costumes. The dressing-room was suddenly filled with costumes of every colour and style. But to Lucy Jane her dress seemed the loveliest.

Lucy Jane was standing in the corridor hoping that Miss Sweetfoot would arrive before the competition started. Miss Sweetfoot could always make her feel relaxed and give her confidence.

Suddenly Lucy Jane heard the sound of a little half whistle coming along the corridor and she was sure it was Miss Sweetfoot, so she rushed along the passage to meet her.

'Oh, Miss Sweetfoot,' she said happily.

Miss Sweetfoot was clasping a bundle of music and looking a little dishevelled. She stopped her little whistle and said, 'Oh dear, oh dear, I thought I'd never get here, I was so worried that you wouldn't have your solo music,' and she greeted Lucy Jane with a little kiss.

Lucy Jane pulled her by the arm. 'I'm in here. I'm nearly ready and I expect Jasmine is changing somewhere else.'

'Now remember,' Miss Sweetfoot said, 'not too much make-up, simple neat hair, and remember, don't wear your watch or your glasses!' She laughed, and Lucy Jane laughed too.

A few minutes later a tall woman and a rather worried-looking man, both in green blazers and carrying long lists pinned to clipboards, started to make their way from dressing-room to dressing-room telling the children the timetable for the day.

'We just want to remind you that in the first section, all children should wear leotard and tights. Then this afternoon each child enters Group Two for the solos and must wear the fancy-dress costume. Tomorrow any child getting into the finals will only need to bring that costume.'

'I didn't know we may be here tomorrow,' Lucy Jane said.

By now the dressing-room was packed with

teachers, mothers and children crammed into every corner, trying to dress or be dressed, doing hair and combing out ringlets and curls and some putting on far too much make-up.

Lucy Jane was already dressed, so she finished tying the ribbon around her neat bun on top of her head and skipped out of the room to find Angela.

'Have you seen Mary Ellen?' she asked. 'I thought she was going to be in your dressing-room.'

'There's another big room along the corridor for all the girls they couldn't fit into these rooms. I expect she's in there with Jasmine,' Angela replied.

'Come with me, Ange,' she called to Angela.

When the two girls put their heads round the door of the next big dressing-room, and Mary Ellen and Jasmine saw them, they let out a scream of delight. At last, they were all together on the big day and all wearing their bracelets!

'Lucy Jane, one girl told me that this stage is very noisy for ballet and you need to step as softly as you can, otherwise you'll be disqualified,' Mary Ellen said.

'Thanks for warning me.'

'And,' Jasmine added, 'they say it's the kind of stage you think you're going to fall off, as there aren't any footlights or things at the front, and you need to use a lot of resin on your feet so you don't slip.'

'How do you know all this?' Angela and Lucy Jane asked, surprised.

'We heard the girl who was in the Junior competiton yesterday tell her sister.'

The four girls looked at each other, concerned.

'Then let's go and have a look,' Angela suggested.

When they walked out on to the large platform they all gave a little gasp of amazement. The huge round auditorium stretched right up into a large glass dome in the centre of the very, very high ceiling. There were boxes in tiers all round the hall, painted in red and gold. Lucy Jane thought at least four thousand people could sit there, and she said as they gingerly stepped forward to get a better look, 'We'll look like mice on this stage.'

'That's true,' Jasmine agreed, 'or maybe ants,' and she laughed.

Lucy Jane didn't feel like laughing. Suddenly she was really nervous.

When the girls started to try out one or two steps, a voice from the stalls called, 'Leave the stage at once, please,' and they all scampered terrified back to their dressing-room before they got into more trouble.

'That was a near thing,' Angela said. She'd enjoyed the danger.

'Yes, but I think we'll stay where we're told to stay from now on,' Mary Ellen replied. 'We don't want to be disqualified and sent home before the dancing's begun.'

When the four girls arrived safely back at Lucy Jane's dressing-room they all stopped and looked at each other, a little secret smile on their faces. They were happy. Even if they didn't win they were just happy and excited to be there, with all the chatter and the togetherness. Lucy Jane suddenly felt she wanted to hold the Russian ballerina's ballet shoes and she quietly knelt down and took them from her case and gave them a little stroke before she neatly put them away again.

But then they were suddenly being pushed and hustled into groups at the side of the stage. Miss Sweetfoot joined them and gave each of them a word of advice, and then she handed the music to the most senior of her girls in each group. 'I'll be out front rooting for you,' she said, smiling, before she left.

Then they were told to wait at the entrance to the stage with their music. They must be ready to dance when their numbers were called. Each of the girls went to use the resin box and swivelled their feet in the crunchy sticky granules to stop them slipping. Some of the girls had green eye shadow, black eye make-up and too much powder and lipstick. They looked like girls that had suddenly grown old.

'That's why Miss Sweetfoot doesn't want us to wear too much make-up,' Lucy Jane thought.

Many of the girls had ringlets and fluffed out curls and some even wore wigs and earrings and looked as if they were in the circus or going to a fancy-dress party rather than a dancing competition.

Once they had found their places at the entrance to the stage, the girls chatted excitedly in little groups, until one of the organisers shouted, 'Silence please. Otherwise you'll be heard on stage.' He screamed so loudly that Lucy Jane jumped and was sure that he must have been heard himself.

Angela, in her low voice, was heard saying, 'Let's get this first silly dance over otherwise we can never have our lunch.' All the girls giggled and an official gave Angela a fierce look. For some reason, two of the girls giggled so hysterically that they had to be taken away and given a glass of water to calm down their nerves.

Suddenly, the girls heard the first competitors' music and Lucy Jane and Jasmine clasped hands nervously as they knew they would be the next. Mary Ellen and Angela were in the third group. All too soon someone called for Lucy Jane's group.

Lucy Jane thought her heart was going to shoot straight out of her body she was so scared. She dipped her toes into the resin box again and took a deep breath, touched the chain round her neck and whispered, 'Good luck, Jasmine,' and then all the girls in Group Two trouped neatly on stage to do their basic

ballet demonstration, which was mainly the exercises they did in class.

There was plenty of room on stage for them to spread out but two of the girls, numbers 16 and 18, rushed to the front so the judges could see them best. When the music began the girls danced in groups of four for the exercises and set routine, which they had all learnt at school. Afterwards each child had to do a short solo. When Lucy Jane had to do hers, she got carried away and suddenly began to enjoy dancing on stage at the Albert Hall and, as Miss Tamara had said she had promise, she added a few extra pirouettes and arm movements which looked very good, although they certainly weren't part of the dance. When they had all finished their solos all the girls from the group rushed very hot and excited back under the stage to change and have their lunch, while they waited for the next two groups to have their turn.

The moment had arrived for each girl to do her two-minute solo in her costume. The excitement was almost too much for some of the girls and the atmosphere in the dressing-room was electric, as the girls struggled into their clothes and huddled in corners practising their steps.

Jasmine was dressed early and looked wonderful in her red, black and white sequinned top hat and tails, so she went to Lucy Jane's dressing-room and helped her to do up her ballet dress and clip the flowers in her hair.

'You look like a picture,' Jasmine said, admiring

Lucy Jane's three-quarter length ballet dress.

'You look great, too,' Lucy Jane replied smiling, and the two girls ran off to wait for their call to do their solos. While Lucy Jane stood waiting to go on stage, rubbing her feet in the resin tin, the two girls who had been so pushy in the exercise section announced they were going to be sick, so they were taken to the cloakroom. Lucy Jane felt frightened, but she remembered what her mother had told her that morning. 'I've got to think I'm going to be good and I will be.' She pulled back her shoulders, checked her number was correctly pinned to her costume and waited, heart beating fast.

The next thing she knew the music was taken from her hand and she was told to go on stage. All summer she had practised, each night she had thought about it, and now the great moment had arrived. The judges sitting in the stalls before her watched her walk gracefully on to the stage and take her place to start her dance. Her music started and suddenly she wasn't frightened. Whether she won a prize or not, this was a moment she would treasure all her life, dancing in a beautiful new ballet dress on stage at the Albert Hall. As she finished her solo she wondered if her mother was there, but when the applause began she was sure she could hear her mother say, 'Well done, Lucy,' so she knew she was. She curtsied and left the stage as gracefully as she could, leaving the judges to discuss her performance and give her marks.

She rushed into the dressing-room to ask Jasmine how her tap dance had gone. 'Not too bad,' Jasmine said smiling, secretly feeling that it had gone rather well.

'Good,' Lucy Jane said happily, relieved that the dance was over. 'Now we're finished, let's change and see if we can watch Mary Ellen and Angela from the side.'

'Great idea,' Jasmine agreed and the two girls rushed

115

to change and put their clothes away neatly before going to watch Angela and Mary Ellen.

By the time they found a place Angela was already finishing her dance. But Lucy Jane and Jasmine still cheered her loudly as she did her little bow, and walked smiling from the stage. When she saw Lucy Jane and Jasmine cheering her she gave a little wave and stuck her tongue out, but luckily the judges couldn't see.

The next competitor was Mary Ellen. She looked very pale and worried as she walked with difficulty on to the stage to place her swords in position. But once the music began her face lit up, her sweet personality glowed and her feet moved like quicksilver.

'She's so good,' Lucy Jane said to Jasmine. 'Better than anyone. No one would ever know she has a bad leg.'

'Yes, she's really good,' Jasmine agreed.

When Mary Ellen finished there was a big burst of applause and Mary Ellen picked up her swords, took her bow and left the stage smiling. Her cheeks were bright pink and she rushed nervously to find the other girls under the stage. When the girls were all united backstage, they huddled anxiously together holding hands waiting for the results. Finally they were told that an announcement would be made at 5 p.m. to say which girls would be needed the following day. In the meantime there was tea for all the competitors in the large canteen backstage.

'How many prizes are there?' one girl asked as they arrived at the canteen.

'About six or ten,' another girl answered.

'Let's hope there are enough to go round,' Angela said. 'One for me, one for Lucy Jane, one for Jasmine and one for Mary Ellen,' and she laughed.

Then all the girls laughed. That would be a dream come true.

At that moment Miss Sweetfoot, who had been watching from the stalls, came rushing into the room. She rushed up to her two pupils, and embraced them enthusiastically.

'I just want to say,' she said with tears in her eyes, 'that both Jasmine and Lucy Jane and your two beautiful sword-dancing friends here,' she indicated Mary Ellen and Angela, 'danced absolutely beautifully and whether or not you win a prize or are called back again tomorrow I couldn't have been more proud of you. Of my eight pupils who are here today, you two have made me the most proud.'

This made the girls so happy that they stopped worrying whether they would be called back the following day. They enjoyed their tea and their success so far.

12

The Results

As the minutes passed and the girls waited in the canteen, one thought kept creeping into their heads: would they be called back tomorrow? Strains of music wafted down from the stage, a reminder that a decision still could not be made as the final group was yet to dance. Lucy Jane found she couldn't eat. Angela only sipped her orange juice absent-mindedly while Mary Ellen and Jasmine looked gloomily at each other dreading the announcement. Miss Sweetfoot looked at all the girls sympathetically. 'Cheer up,' she said. 'I'll go and see what's happening.'

She hadn't been gone long when a man with a clipboard marched into the room and called, 'The following girls are to come back tomorrow.' As Lucy Jane, Jasmine, Mary Ellen and Angela were all among the names on the list they hugged each other happily.

At home that night Lucy Jane found it impossible to sleep. She went to the window and looked out. As she looked up at the dark sky and gazed at the stars twinkling over the house, she named the stars after each of her friends. 'If none of us win, we're all stars anyway,' she said to herself. When she got back into bed the music for her dance went round and round in her head until finally she fell into a deep sleep until morning. She woke fresh and rested for the final day. She felt as though something lovely was going to happen and instead of being nervous she couldn't wait to get back to the Albert Hall and dance again.

Because it was the finals day there were only half the number of girls there. The atmosphere was not so jolly and everyone seemed rather silent and serious.

Lucy Jane kept trying to think positively. 'I'm going to be good, I'm going to be good,' she said over and over again, as she changed into her ballet dress ready to do her solo.

Lucy Jane's solo was the same one she had danced the day before and was in waltz time.

She had wanted to dance a polka, but Miss Sweetfoot had said now she was older she should dance to a waltz, as it would give her more opportunity to use soft, graceful movements, show off her stretch and *arabesques*, *pirouettes* and *grands jetés*. The middle section of the dance was in double time which allowed Lucy Jane's neat footwork, well-pointed toes and *entrechats* to be seen to advantage.

Lucy Jane loved the dance. She didn't notice that the pianist was not really playing her music very well, and she danced with a special joy and sparkle, which many of the girls in the competition did not have. She brought with her a glow and love of dance which lit up the stage and made her a pleasure to watch.

119

Suddenly Miss Tamara's words, 'I expect to see you dance in Russia', were going round in her head, she felt dizzy with pleasure and the happiness of having danced as well as she could. If it felt like this to dance at Covent Garden every night, Lucy Jane knew she would love it, even if it would be hard work.

Each girl's turn seemed to be over incredibly quickly, and before the girls knew it they were all sitting and waiting nervously for the results, and grumbling about the pianist and all the wrong notes she had played. Then there was a curious hush in the dressing-room, and the girls all looked very gloomy as though they were waiting to walk the plank. Suddenly the door was flung open and the official announced: 'All girls on stage, please.'

In a panic all the girls hurried to the stage and stood side by side in their costumes, their hearts beating fast and their hands hot and sticky with excitement.

Then one of the famous judges in the auditorium rose to make a little speech from the front of the stalls. 'That's Linda Lanton, the ballerina,' one of the girls whispered.

'I know it is,' the girl next to her replied.

Miss Lanton started her speech.

'As I am sure you know,' she said in a high clear voice, 'there are four cups, four runner-up prizes and four highly commended certificates.' She took a deep breath and then said slowly, 'We want you to know that in our eyes all the girls who have performed here today are winners in their own way, because the standard of dancing has been exceptionally high.' There was a short pause, and she said, 'Now before the star of the Paris Ballet, Serge Signoret, reads out the winners, I have one word to say from the judges on make-up. We all felt that in general you wore too much make-up. You are all very pretty and don't really need much. Remember we are here to see you dance and too much make-up is distracting.' Mary Ellen and Lucy Jane were relieved they hadn't put too much on, and so was Jasmine who had wanted to wear gold eye-shadow.

Then a tall, dark-haired, good-looking young man in a black velvet suit stood up.

'The winner of the Gold Ballet Cup is Sandra Galley.'

There was a round of applause and Lucy Jane felt a little lead weight of disappointment in her heart.

'Next, the winner of the Gold Tap and Modern Cup is Jasmine Beckles.'

Lucy Jane screamed with delight and jumped up and down and kissed Jasmine before she went to receive her cup.

'Next, the winner of the Gold Scottish and National Dancing Cup is Mary Ellen Foster.'

Again, Lucy Jane and the group of girls cheered. They were so happy Mary Ellen had won.

'And finally, the Gold Star Performance Cup goes to . . .'

There was a pause as Serge Signoret had dropped the piece of paper and had to fumble about on the floor to find it.

'Sorry,' he said when he got up and stroked his dark black hair into place. 'Sorry,' he said again, looking at the paper. 'The Gold Cup for Star Performance goes to three girls who have exceptional talent in very different ways. They are Jacqueline Jones . . .'

Everyone applauded. Lucy Jane and Angela looked at each other and shrugged, a little wry smile on their faces. Their chance of a prize had almost gone. Then Monsieur Signoret announced, '*and Angela Davies* . . .'

Lucy Jane and Mary Ellen and Jasmine were thrilled. Then Serge Signoret said, 'And last, but not least, Lucy Jane Tadworth. These three girls share the Gold Cup for Star Performance.'

Lucy Jane couldn't believe her ears.

Tears came to her eyes. She thought she was dreaming as she walked up in a daze to receive the cup with Angela and Jacqueline Jones.

'Young ladies,' Serge Signoret said in a whisper, 'you will all have to share the cup today but a replica will be sent in a few days.'

The girls smiled and nodded.

After the girls had received their prizes they stood in a haze of happiness, not hearing the names of the other eight girls who collected their certificates and prizes.

In the dressing-room the girls hugged each other. Their dream had come true, they had all surprised themselves and become stars for a moment. Now it was back to normal life and work, but they would all try

123

and persuade their parents to let them go to the
dancing camp next year.

At that moment Mr and Mrs Tadworth, Mr and Mrs
Beckles and Mr and Mrs Foster and Mrs Davies burst
into the room full of smiles to congratulate their
daughters. 'Oh, it was so wonderful. You were all so
good,' the mothers said at once, their eyes brimming
with tears.

The girls threw themselves into their parents' arms.
Mr Tadworth and Mr Beckles smiled proudly. Then

Mr Tadworth suddenly suggested, 'I know, to celebrate the success of our clever little daughters, let's take them to a Chinese restaurant and have a celebration meal.'

The girls were thrilled at the idea. 'What about Miss Sweetfoot?' Lucy Jane asked.

'She can come too,' her father answered.

So the girls packed up their clothes as quickly as they could and went to look for Miss Sweetfoot.

Miss Sweetfoot was waiting outside the door, a huge grin on her face and four red roses in her hand. 'These are for the four new stars,' she said as she handed each girl a rose. 'You were all brilliant.'

At that moment more girls and their parents pushed into the dressing-room making a terrible squash. 'Come on,' Mr Tadworth said, 'I think everyone is wonderful including you, Miss Sweetfoot,' and he gave her a little hug. 'Let's go and toast champagne to the girls' success.'

So they all made their way from the Albert Hall, plus suitcases, dresses, roses and prizes to enjoy a celebration dinner.

Lucy Jane held her rose in one hand and Miss Tamara's ballet shoes in the other. Angela was carrying their gold cup and waving it above her head.

Lucy Jane looked at it and smiled. Was this the beginning of her career as a ballet dancer? She would write to Miss Tamara. She touched the cup for a second and said quietly, 'We won, we all won.'

The first two Lucy Jane books are:

LUCY JANE ON TELEVISION

Lucy Jane is a little wary of spending a holiday alone with her grandmother in Scotland. But when she sees in the local paper that a TV company is looking for girls to star in a costume drama she is determined to get the part – though it's not quite as simple as she first thinks . . .

and

LUCY JANE AT THE BALLET

When Lucy Jane's mother has to go into hospital, Lucy Jane is sent to stay with her Aunt Sarah. She is most reluctant to go, she wants to stay at home with her father and her cat, Tilly.

But Lucy Jane doesn't realise what surprises lie in store for her, for Aunt Sarah is wardrobe mistress at the Theatre Royal, Covent Garden and Lucy Jane is swiftly drawn into the life of a ballet company.

A selected list of titles available from Mammoth

While every effort is made to keep prices low, it is sometimes necessary to increase prices at short notice. Mandarin Paperbacks reserves the right to show new retail prices on covers which may differ from those previously advertised in the text or elsewhere.

The prices shown below were correct at the time of going to press.

☐	7497 0366 0	**Dilly the Dinosaur**	Tony Bradman	£2.50
☐	7497 0137 4	**Flat Stanley**	Jeff Brown	£2.50
☐	7497 0306 7	**The Chocolate Touch**	P Skene Catling	£2.50
☐	7497 0568 X	**Dorrie and the Goblin**	Patricia Coombs	£2.50
☐	7497 0114 5	**Dear Grumble**	W J Corbett	£2.50
☐	7497 0054 8	**My Naughty Little Sister**	Dorothy Edwards	£2.50
☐	7497 0723 2	**The Little Prince (colour ed.)**	A Saint-Exupery	£3.99
☐	7497 0305 9	**Bill's New Frock**	Anne Fine	£2.99
☐	7497 0590 6	**Wild Robert**	Diana Wynne Jones	£2.50
☐	7497 0661 9	**The Six Bullerby Children**	Astrid Lindgren	£2.50
☐	7497 0319 9	**Dr Monsoon Taggert's Amazing Finishing Academy**	Andrew Matthews	£2.50
☐	7497 0420 9	**I Don't Want To!**	Bel Mooney	£2.50
☐	7497 0833 6	**Melanie and the Night Animal**	Gillian Rubinstein	£2.50
☐	7497 0264 8	**Akimbo and the Elephants**	A McCall Smith	£2.50
☐	7497 0048 3	**Friends and Brothers**	Dick King-Smith	£2.50
☐	7497 0795 X	**Owl Who Was Afraid of the Dark**	Jill Tomlinson	£2.99

All these books are available at your bookshop or newsagent, or can be ordered direct from the publisher. Just tick the titles you want and fill in the form below.

Mandarin Paperbacks, Cash Sales Department, PO Box 11, Falmouth, Cornwall TR10 9EN.

Please send cheque or postal order, no currency, for purchase price quoted and allow the following for postage and packing:

UK including BFPO
£1.00 for the first book, 50p for the second and 30p for each additional book ordered to a maximum charge of £3.00.

Overseas including Eire
£2 for the first book, £1.00 for the second and 50p for each additional book thereafter.

NAME (Block letters) ....

ADDRESS ....

....

☐ I enclose my remittance for ....

☐ I wish to pay by Access/Visa Card Number

Expiry Date
